THE LONG

DARK NIGHT

THE SEVEN SISTERS
SERIES

CAHIRA O'DONNELL

The Long Dark Night
A Dark River Publishing Book / June 2013

Published by Dark River Publishing
A Division of Path Home, LLC
Berthoud, Colorado

This is a work of Fiction. Names, characters, places, and incidents are either the product of the author's imagination or are used fictitiously, and any resemblance to actual persons, living or dead, events, or locales is entirely coincidental.

ISBN: 978-0615807973

For my Children

Whose undying faith and love

Make everything possible

With Deep Gratitude

To my Associate Publishing Specialist, Trixie Phelps, whose "preparation for publication" magic has brought this story from the ethers into ordinary reality.

To my editor, Cody Alexander, and proof reader, Terry Lamond, whose dedication and laborious attention to detail have made this work readable.

THE LONG DARK NIGHT

Dark River Publishing
PO Box 8
Berthoud, CO 80513

~ CHAPTER ONE ~

The house was under siege. A van filled with a uniformed SWAT team pulled up. Armed to the gills, officers poured out and surrounded her house. Four unmarked Blackhawk helicopters landed in the open field across the street. Road blocks sectioned off her neighborhood. Black Hummers and special operations forces converged upon the house, and a black, bulletproof limo pulled into the drive. Three men in dark suits, dark glasses, and backed by special ops in black, unmarked uniforms, approached the front door. It was obviously a military operation, but nothing in their appearance gave away what branch.

Talia Martin sat straight and composed on her living room couch, idly watching the activity through her front window. She was really quite surprised it had taken them this long to come for her. The news about the captured Navy Seals had hit the internet several hours ago. She'd had time to shower, dress and have toast and tea before they descended upon her in force. She wore a straight, black knit skirt that ended just above her knees, a pearl gray silk shell topped with a matching cashmere cardigan sweater, and black pumps. Her naturally platinum blonde hair was done up in a classic French roll. A black leather tote, packed and ready, was sitting next to her couch. She didn't need so much as a change of clothes. They knew her size.

The doorbell chimed and she calmly got up and opened the front door. One of the special ops swept inside, sidearm drawn with the barrel held upward, to secure the premises. He was followed by a man in a dark suit.

"Miss Martin?"

"Yes."

"I am Agent Adams. By order of the President of the United States, you are being drafted into active duty," one of the suited men informed her, handing her a packet of papers.

"Is there anyone else here, ma'am?" the agent inquired.

"Just my cats. You have made arrangements?"

"Yes, ma'am," another of the three agents answered. "We've brought a house sitter. She has her instructions. Have there been any changes?"

Talia knew the "house sitter" would be an undercover agent.

"I left my keys and written instructions on my desk," Talia softly responded. She hated this, hated leaving her cats, her garden and her little house, her isolated sanctuary. She just wanted to be left alone. Last time they had promised it would be the last, as they had the time before, and the time before that. When she saw the magnitude of the attack and capture of the Seals, however, she simply resigned herself. Young men had already been sent home in boxes; now those sent to retaliate had been taken. Such mud did not sit well on the president's face during an election year. She knew she would be called in. She, who found war abhorrent, would be responsible for more bloodshed, causing death to save life. When would it end?

"Are you ready to go, ma'am?" Agent Adams inquired.

She stood, picked up her tote and walked to the door. One of the special ops approached her, took the tote and started to search it, while another moved in to search her person. She took a deliberate step back from the large man.

"Ensign, stand down. Don't touch her," Adams spoke in a sharp command. "Under no circumstances is she to be touched."

Ensign? Must be Navy, Talia decided. The guard backed off immediately, for which she was eternally grateful. The proximity of so many had her on edge. Agent Adams opened the front door, handed her the tote and indicated she precede him outside. Immediately surrounded by the other two men and special operations personnel, she was quickly escorted to the waiting limo. One agent sat on either side of her and one across. The doors closed, and they were underway.

No one spoke. The limo took her four blocks to the end of the open field where the Blackhawks had landed. She was escorted to the chopper in the middle of the grouping, seated between her dark suited escorts, and the choppers took off in formation.

~ CHAPTER TWO ~

Secret Service Special Agent Nickolas Pane didn't know when he had been more devastated. His kid brother, Navy Seal, Lieutenant Commander Daniel Pane, was MIA, apparently captured by the Taliban in Iraq. Not two hours after receiving the news, his director had called him into headquarters. He took the next available flight from Wyoming to Washington, DC where he met with a CIA Agent. The latter offered him a mysterious proposal – a proposal that gave him an opportunity to play an active role in the possible rescue of his brother and the surviving members of his special ops team. No sooner had he indicated his willingness to do whatever it took, he was air transported from Washington to Fort Stewart, Georgia. Nickolas was puzzled to have been sent to an Army installation, given his brother was a Navy Seal. To his further surprise, instead of barracks, he had been appointed a luxurious suite of rooms where he sat cooling his heels awaiting the arrival of a "special agent," at which time he would be debriefed.

Cooling his heels had never been his strong suit, he decided as he paced back and forth across the living room. At six foot five, his strides were so long that he found himself doing more turning around than pacing, so he decided to sit down – again. He sat for a short time, leg bouncing up and down in agitation and was just about to rise. A knock on the door preceded a Special Forces Team sweeping into the room, followed by three agents surrounding one small, shapely blonde.

"Agent Pane, I am Agent Adams," one of the three addressed him. "This is Miss Talia Martin, sir. You have been assigned as her bodyguard."

Bodyguard? What the hell was this? He was supposed to be helping get his brother back, not babysitting an undersized, over built blonde bombshell. Hell, she was probably some general's plaything, he thought, looking her up and down – taking in her tiny feet clad in black pumps, shapely calves, curvaceous hips, tiny waist and impossibly full breasts.

"Agent Pane," she acknowledged, drawing his attention to her perfectly formed face and cool gray eyes. Holy shit, she was beautiful! Keen intelligence shone from her unusual eyes as they met his in a steady, piercing regard. No, he reevaluated, this woman was no man's plaything.

"Miss Martin," he responded automatically, offering his hand only to have his wrist grabbed by the team member closest to her.

In a lightning fast move, Nickolas performed a release and put the man in an arm lock.

"Sorry, sir, she is not to be touched," the hapless man explained through teeth gritted against the pain of his tortured joints.

Talia was impressed by Agent Pane's unbelievably fast reflexes. He was tall, powerfully built, and she could tell he was honed into a lethal weapon. His thick, dark brown hair was cut military short, drawing attention to high cheek bones and ice cold electric blue eyes. Muscles rippled as he released the man and stood back.

"Neither am I, officer. You would be wise to remember that," his deep, expressionless voice rumbled.

6

"Yes, sir."

Agent Pane was wearing a dark suit rather than a uniform, so she couldn't tell his rank, but it was clearly higher than any of the men in the room who had escorted her, judging from the way they were all standing down. Agent Adams had been treated with deference by military personnel on their trip, giving her a clue that Pane was likely pretty high up in the pecking order.

"Sir, you will both be picked up and escorted to debriefing in thirty minutes," Agent Adams informed them. "Ma'am, a wardrobe has been delivered to your room should you need to change," he said, indicating her damp clothes. It had been raining upon their arrival. "Agent Pane, sir, I take it you are currently unarmed?"

"More or less, yes," Pane responded. He had shipped his Beretta .45 rather than deal with airport security on his commercial flight to DC, and it had not yet been delivered to his quarters. Though he disliked being without it, with his training, he was never really unarmed. His body might as well be registered as a deadly weapon.

Adams reached into his own jacket, pulled out a 9mm Beretta and handed it to him butt first. Pane took it, checked the clip and chamber with efficient movements and then put it into the back of his pants.

"Our orders are that she is to be protected as if you were guarding the President himself, sir."

"I can do that," Pane responded coolly.

"Your personal sidearm and any other weapons of choice will be issued at debriefing, sir," Adams assured him.

Who the hell was the woman that she was being treated like a national treasure? Pane wondered, looking down on her blonde head. She barely reached five foot two, yet she stood in the midst of enough oversized special ops and secret service personnel to guard the oval office, seeming to take it in her stride. The men towered over her small form, crowding but not touching her, he noticed. Her sweater and hair were damp, but otherwise every hair was in place, and she stood stock still, calm and collected. Not a fidget or sign of nerves to be seen. One cool little number.

After searching the rooms and finding them secure, her escort departed, leaving the two of them standing alone in the living room of the suite.

"Which room is mine?" she questioned softly.

"The one on the right," he answered, indicating the larger of the two bedrooms with a tilt of his head.

"Thanks," she said, going into the room he had indicated and closing the door.

Soon he heard a hair dryer running in the room's private bath, so he busied himself breaking down the hand gun. He preferred his older model Beretta .45 to the 9mm, but could manage well with either. While the .45 was bulkier, he liked the larger caliber, and it fit well in his oversized hand. He never left the condition of his weapons up to others, and wasn't about to start now that he was responsible for Miss National Treasure.

She reemerged a short time later, having changed the light gray shell and cardigan for a charcoal, long sleeved silk blouse with pearl buttons. It was neatly tucked into the waistband of her straight black skirt, accentuating her small waist and full breasts. Her hair, now dry, was done up into its former classic French roll, and she had applied fresh tinted lip gloss. He took in her appearance without missing a detail. He made it his business to never miss details; it was part of what made him the best of the best.

"Satisfied?" she asked, aware of his scrutiny. Goose bumps rose on her skin in the wake of his ice blue eyes as his impersonal gaze moved over her.

"Hardly," he responded. What was it about this woman that affected him like no other? Just looking at her had him wanting to mount her – not just have her, but to claim her. He had no use for self absorbed beautiful women. It was unsettling.

"Satisfied enough that it is safe for me to sit down?"

"Please, be my guest." He gathered himself enough to indicate the other chair at the small table where he had just finished field dressing his gun. He snapped the clip back into the butt, chambered a bullet, switched on the safety and put the 9mm into the back of his pants. She sat, crossed one shapely leg over the other and regarded him with cool gray eyes. Neither of them spoke. Soon there was a knock at the door, indicating the escort had arrived to take them to debriefing.

While Nickolas was surprised at the high brass in attendance, Miss National Treasure didn't seem to be impressed. They all sat around a conference table where he held out a chair for Talia, then took up post behind her as her bodyguard.

"You might as well be seated, Agent Pane, this debriefing is for you both," an older man addressed him. Judging by the stars on his uniform, he was a general. Nickolas noted there were also high ranking representatives from the Navy, Air Force and Marines.

"Yes, sir," Nickolas responded, taking the empty seat next to Talia.

"Miss Martin, thank you for, once again, being of service to your country," the general addressed Talia. She silently nodded her head in acknowledgement. The woman's composure was unbelievable, Nickolas observed. If she'd been a man, he would have thought her to have titanium balls.

"Agent Pane is not only assigned as your bodyguard, but he will also serve as your link," the general continued. Again she nodded in silence.

Nickolas, on the other hand, wanted to know what the hell a "link" was. Knowing now was not the time to ask, he remained silent.

"The following information and this entire operation are totally classified. As you both know, a team of Navy Seals has been taken by the Taliban. We have reason to believe there are a number of survivors being held in Iraq. An extraction team has already been deployed and will meet with you upon your arrival. You will receive a preliminary debriefing here, then fly out at 0:600, commercial, undercover as civilians, through a back route. The rest of what you need to know will be given to you en route."

"I take it Agent Pane's son is believed to be among the survivors?" Talia asked the general.

Nickolas noted she did not address the high ranking officer as "sir." She must be a civilian. Then it hit him – son? Christ, how old did she think he was? Sure, at thirty-five he had seen some miles – hard miles if he was to be completely honest, but for Daniel to be his son he would have to have been a father at five.

"No, not his son, his brother. Naturally, we will need you to confirm he is a suitable link before departure."

"Do you have backup links available?"

"Yes, Miss Martin, but Agent Pane is by far the best match on all counts. Also, he is a member of the Secret Service, and from what I can see here, considered one of the best," the general said, consulting the dossier on the table in front of him. "I don't think I have to fill you in on the advantages of working with a professional rather than a civilian."

"Is he aware of the ramifications of serving as a link?"

"Have you been debriefed as to your duties with Miss Martin, Agent Pane?" the general addressed him.

"Only that I am to be her bodyguard, sir."

"I will not move forward until that gross oversight is corrected," Talia informed the room at large, folding her little arms over her not so little breasts in a show of obstinate determination.

Christ, she was facing down a room full of brass as if reprimanding a kindergarten class. Man or not, the woman had a set that hung to her knees.

"Rest assured it will be included in the en route debriefing, Miss Martin. Agent Pane has indicated his willingness to do whatever it takes to regain his brother," the general assured her.

"I will not leave this base with the man, nor will I touch him until he has been fully apprised of what is involved and in absolute, fully informed, voluntary agreement. If you will excuse me, gentlemen." She stood and walked out, hips swaying and high heels clicking smartly on the tile floor. The special forces scrambled to accompany her when she passed through the security doors, as did Nickolas.

"Agent Pane, our men will escort her. Apparently you will be needed for debriefing sooner rather than later." Nickolas was sure he heard wry resignation in the general's voice. What in the hell was going on here that one small civilian woman had an entire room of brass dancing to her tune? Hell, unless he missed his guess, which he was not in the habit of doing, she couldn't be much over twenty-five.

~ CHAPTER THREE ~

When Nickolas returned to their quarters, his head was spinning. He could hardly credit what he had learned of the indomitable Miss Martin. Had it not come from the most reliable sources in the country, had he not been shown her track record, he wouldn't have believed it. Apparently, she was a gifted psychic, for lack of a better term, that had been instrumental in numerous dangerous top secret operations involving various branches of the military. She had been brought in on this operation under the orders of the President himself. If all he had been told was true, he would have her under lock and key, rather than living alone as a civilian between operations. If even half of it was true, she was indeed a national treasure and a dangerous weapon should she be taken and used against them.

Then there was the little issue of his role as link. Apparently, she was able to contact captives through a male relative if the DNA was a close enough match and the link's brain waves were compatible with hers. That explained the medical tests he had been submitted to before being shipped out. He was also apprised that, in the past, her links did not fare so well. There was reportedly something about working with Miss Martin in that capacity which created obsessions in the men she worked with. Several had to be arrested for stalking her, and three others had eventually committed suicide. Not that he was overly concerned about that. Sure, she was cute – damned cute – fucking gorgeous – if he were to be honest with himself, but he doubted he would lose his head over her. He never lost his head over a woman. Even if he did become attached to her, he was a strong man. He wasn't about to stalk a woman that had no interest in him, much less "off" himself when she rejected him. Besides, he was a professional. He never got involved with the women he was assigned to guard.

When he stepped into the suite, he found her working on a small laptop. She looked up at him with those piercing gray eyes.

"Am I to take it they were unable to scare you off?" she asked in an ironic tone.

"I don't scare easily."

"Then you are either a complete fool or you love your brother very much."

"I would die for him," he stated simply.

"Before this is over, you very well may wish you had," she informed him in a sad, resigned voice, turning back to her laptop. "Are you married?" she surprised him by asking.

"No."

"In a serious relationship?"

"No."

"Well, at least there's that. They're waiting for us at the lab." She closed a file and folded the computer shut. "We might as well get this over with. I've been informed our flight is an early one, so we'll need our rest," she said as she stood and headed for the door.

They were escorted to a medical facility on the base and directed to a room full of equipment, personnel in lab coats, and numerous men in uniform. Several of them were familiar to

Nickolas. He identified them as military intelligence he'd worked with in the past.

"So you got rooked into it again?" a tall Army officer addressed Talia as they entered the lab.

"Hello, Dr. Wilkinson, so nice to see you again," she greeted him, affection clear in her voice. Nickolas noticed that, though they seemed to know each other well, neither reached to shake hands.

"Will this be first contact?" the doctor wanted to know.

"Yes, I thought it best to wait until we were here."

"Probably wise," the doctor agreed, looking Nickolas up and down. "Agent Pane, I take it?"

"Yes, sir."

"Have you been fully debriefed as to your work with Miss Martin?"

"Yes, sir."

"And you are willing to take the risks involved?"

"Yes, sir, I am."

"Well then, let's get started," he said, directing Nickolas to a chair. Talia sat down in one directly across from him, and medical personnel began putting various monitors on them both. He noticed Talia openly flinched when one med-tech's fingers brushed her arm as he attached the blood pressure cuff. The aide's eyes widened, color draining from his face at the contact.

"You were informed of the importance of gloves and avoiding direct contact, were you not?" Dr. Wilkinson demanded.

"Yes, sir." The man's voice shook, and he couldn't take his eyes off of Talia.

"Escort this man to psychiatric, and send in a replacement," Wilkinson ordered. The med-tech was immediately taken from the room by security, and another took his place.

"My deep apologies, Miss Martin. Are you well enough to proceed?" the doctor asked. She simply nodded.

What in the hell was that about? Nickolas wondered.

"Agent Pane, you are to hold perfectly still, keeping your hands on the arms of your chair. Miss Martin will touch the back of your right hand with her fingers. Let us know when it becomes too intense for you, and we will give you a break. Do you understand?"

"I understand your instructions, yes." Nickolas said. He didn't understand much more than that but chose not to expound.

Talia took a deep fortifying breath and looked him in the eyes. He didn't think it possible, but her eyes appeared to glow, developing multiple, sparkling facets like gray diamonds.

"What is your brother's name?" she asked softly.

"Daniel, Daniel Pane," Nickolas responded, voice thickening in emotion.

"Please think of him for me," she requested quietly. Talia waited for his nod indicating he had done so, then touched his right hand with the fore and middle finger of her left.

He nearly came off of his chair. Lust slammed into him like a freight train, and he couldn't find his next breath. He looked into her eyes in shock. What he saw there was a poignant mixture of apology, regret and – pain. OMG! WTF? His substantial cock was at full attention trying to find its way out of his pants, and all he could think of was getting into hers. Then, to his utter amazement, he watched bruises form on her perfect face and her eyes shift to green, the exact green of his brother's. Her soft lower lip became swollen and then split, and her breathing began to rasp. A pain filled moan escaped her mouth, but it was pitched too low to be hers.

"Are you an angel?" his brother's voice asked through her.

"No, Daniel," she answered in her own voice, "I'm with your brother, Nickolas. We're trying to find you. Do you know where you are?"

"No, I was blindfolded, but we were transported by ground for no more than three hours. We can't be too far from where we were taken," his voice answered through her. "You must be an angel; I can see your light. Am I dying? Have you come to take me?"

"That's just the way I am appearing in your mind, Daniel. What you see is my astral body."

"Nice body," he responded.

Nickolas was in full agreement with his brother's assessment. He was convinced if he didn't get into that gorgeous body soon, he would explode. He bit the inside of his mouth trying to hold out in order to maintain contact with his brother.

"Her vitals are fluctuating, blood pressure dropping. We need to break contact," one of the medics informed the doctor.

"No." The command came through Talia in her voice. "It's his injuries, not mine. His rib has been broken and punctured a lung," she broke off in a liquid, wracking cough. "I need to stay long enough to take it on, or we'll lose him." Blood seeped out of her mouth, and her breathing became increasingly labored.

"Talia, release him now," Dr. Wilkinson ordered.

"No," she whispered, gripping Nickolas' wrist in desperation. "Don't let them separate us, don't leave me, or your brother will die," she implored, looking at him through his brother's green eyes out of her battered face. She gurgled, "Nickolas, help me," in his brother's agonized voice. At her request, Nickolas laced his fingers through hers and held on tight.

"Prepare a transfusion, get me suction!" The doctor started shouting orders as medics scrambled.

~

Daniel had been lying on a hard dirt floor in fevered agony, drifting in and out of consciousness when his angel came for him. She floated just out of reach, white-blonde hair flowing around her bare shoulders and down her back, diamond eyes shining out of an ethereal face. She was the most beautiful woman he had ever seen. He wanted her. Even through his agony he wanted her. If this was what could be found in heaven, he was more than ready. He knew he'd never survive another beating. Hell, he was relatively sure he wasn't going to survive the last one. He could hear the rattle in his lungs and knew they were filling. He was drowning in his own blood, rapidly running out of time with no help in sight.

She spoke to him, though he couldn't remember all she had said. She'd covered his agonized body with her own. He could almost feel her velvet skin and silken hair as her mouth covered his, giving him breath. Then the damnedest thing happened. Her body literally sank into his, and he had the orgasm of his life. To die for! he thought in wry humor, as orgasm after orgasm wracked his tortured body. With each release, the pain faded and breathing became easier until he finally felt her drift out and away.

He lay there shuddering for quite some time before he gathered himself enough to make an assessment. His mind was clearing, he was no longer drowning, the pain was gone, but her memory remained – her memory and the post orgasmic shudders that still wracked his body.

~

Talia lost consciousness and pitched forward in her chair. Nickolas released her hand, caught her, swept her up into his arms and deposited her on the gurney that had been rushed in. He watched in amazement as the medical staff fought for her life.

"Do we need to prepare her for surgery?" a medic asked the doctor.

"No, we just need to stabilize her until she can repair the damage herself," Dr. Wilkinson responded.

Repair it herself? She was a mess! Furthermore, Nickolas had no idea how she had gotten that way. The damage mysteriously showed up as she sat in that damned chair sounding like his brother. There wasn't much that shook Agent Pane. He was known as "Ice Man" under fire, but he was shaken now. In disbelief, he watched the bruises slowly fade from her pale face, her lip repair itself and her breathing return to normal.

Her hair had come out of the French roll and flowed around her like a platinum shroud. She looked like a fairy child in eternal sleep. He wanted her with every fiber of his being.

~ CHAPTER FOUR ~

They'd kept her overnight in the medical facility under observation, and he had returned to their assigned quarters. Being apart from her was an agony he did not understand. For god's sake, he didn't even know the woman. Yet, every time he closed his eyes, there she was, helpless and unconscious on the gurney. It was all he could do not to go back and demand to see her, to hold her to his chest and be sure she still lived, to cover her luscious mouth with his and breathe his own life into her if need be. Yes, Ice Man Pane was shaken to his core.

It was quite clear to him that she had somehow saved his brother's life. He had no idea how, but he saw what he saw, and it was his brother's eyes and voice coming through her. It had to have been his brother's injuries she took on.

By 04:30 the next morning, it had been a restless night, long on thoughts and short on sleep. As per orders, he was up, dressed and packed, though how they were expected to travel with her in the condition she had been in when he last saw her, he had no idea. He was distracted from his thoughts when a knock sounded on the door and an aide entered.

"I have come for Miss Martin's luggage. Your shuttle to the airport leaves in forty minutes, sir," he informed Pane.

"We're still flying out?"

"Yes, sir, you are due to pick Miss Martin up at the med center in about fifteen minutes," the aide responded. "Can I help you with your luggage as well?"

"Yeah, thanks," he agreed, "all I have is that duffel." Normally he would have refused help as he traveled light, but with his duties as bodyguard, he needed to keep his hands free.

When he entered the hospital room, he was surprised to see her sitting straight and still as if nothing had happened. He was also stunned by the lust that slammed into him without warning.

She looked fresh and rested in a peach silk blouse and light tan linen suit. The skirt hugged her hips, ending just above her knees, with a pleated panel in back. She wore matching tan pumps, and her hair was up in the damned French roll. Gone was the fairy, replaced by Miss National Treasure, he thought, as she regarded him with those cool, unreadable gray eyes.

"Agent Pane," she greeted with a regal tilt of her head.

"Miss Martin," he responded. "You look well rested."

She did not elect to reply. Instead, she sat calm and contained, legs crossed, arms on the rests of the chair, well-manicured hands relaxed and still. He looked down at those hands. Her nails were moderately long, and her polish matched her blouse. How in the hell had she managed that on a military base, when several hours ago, she was unconscious on a gurney, with a punctured lung? For that matter, how the hell had she managed the punctured lung in the first place?

"Thank you, Agent Samuels, I can take over now," he addressed the Secret Service Agent that had been assigned to his team. The tall, dark-skinned Samuels quietly stood behind her at a respectful distance.

"Yes, sir," Samuels responded, and promptly left.

"Are you ready to go to the airport?" he asked her, still not believing she could be totally recovered.

"Yes," she replied. Picking up a tan leather hand bag from beside her chair, she preceded him to the door of the hospital room where special operations personnel stood at attention on either side.

The two special ops fell in behind them, escorted them to the lobby of the hospital and directly out front where an unmarked black limo awaited them. Agent Samuels was already seated in front next to the driver when one of the officers opened the back door. Talia slid in, followed by Nickolas.

Talia watched the huge agent out of the side of her eye as he folded his massive frame into the seat next to her. He was very impressive in his dark suit and mirrored sunglasses. She wondered how tall he really was. He was so strongly built and well-proportioned, it was hard to tell, but she guessed him to be at least six four or five. All told, he appeared to be holding up well. After their first encounter, most links were visibly shaken. He had even witnessed her channel his brother, take on and heal his injuries. Grown men had been known to faint dead away with much less exposure to her little idiosyncrasies, she thought with self-deprecating humor. Most were at least wary, giving her wide birth while devouring her with distrustful, lust filled eyes.

Agent Pane did neither. He appeared professional and contained. Though she couldn't see his eyes behind the reflective lenses, she could tell he was in bodyguard status, taking note of their environment rather than ogling her.

"I take it you are rather high ranking in the Secret Service," Talia stated. She had noted that more called him "sir" than not.

"I am, yes."

"So, babysitting me must feel a bit beneath you."

"No, not at all." He would like to have her beneath him, he thought.

Did she actually see his lips twitch in humor?

"How so?"

He looked down at her in silence for a time. She could see her own reflection in the lenses of his dark glasses.

"Let's just say I've seen what you're capable of and am smart enough to connect the dots."

"What do you mean?"

"Miss Martin, you are undoubtedly the greatest asset we have on this mission. You would also be the greatest detriment in the wrong hands. I consider you of utmost importance to national security and am highly motivated to see you have the best protection available," he told her after glancing at the bullet and sound proof glass between the front seat and the back where they sat to assure their privacy.

"And that would be you?"

"That would be me, yes."

She looked into his dark glasses for the longest time, then turned her attention to the window next to her. She sat still and poised, saying nothing more. Upon "reading" him, it became clear this man was a natural born hero, an exceptional alpha warrior of great integrity, top in his class. God, how she hated destroying him.

~ CHAPTER FIVE ~

When they reached the airport in Savannah, GA, airport security escorted them across the polished granite main floor and through security via the pilot's lane without being scanned or searched. She had no doubt Agents Pane and Samuels were armed. Apparently, provisions had been made to keep it that way. Sandwiched between the two giants, she felt even smaller than usual. Even with her two and a half inch heels, she barely reached either man's shoulder. Agent Pane was several inches taller than Samuels, bigger boned and more densely muscled, while Samuels, tall, dark and swarthy, was no slouch.

Agent Samuels left them at the gate where they were the last to board the US Airways flight. The flight attendant escorted Agent Pane and Talia to their first class seats. Pane indicated she should take the window seat, leaving him to sit on the aisle. Even with only two seats in the row and first class leg room, he had to leave his legs in the aisle. Yes, at least six-five, she decided.

The flight had been underway for less than an hour when they had finished a light but most welcomed breakfast. Nickolas had read the debriefing on the mission as well as the information on Miss National Treasure and was absorbing all he had learned. Said treasure sat looking out the window in silence. How could someone be that still for so long? In his experience, women tended to twitch, primp and run off at the mouth at every opportunity – but not Miss Martin. She was so still, inside and out, that even his finely honed senses could hardly detect her presence.

Too bad his damned cock didn't have the same problem. It was in a constant state of aching arousal, more than aware of her soft body seated next to him. He'd once found a male dog that had strangled itself on its own chain trying to get at a bitch in heat. That was exactly how he felt, like he was strangling himself on his own restraint.

"I understand you were born with your abilities," he said, breaking the silence.

"Yes," she replied, not looking away from the window.

"Have you been trained in the use of them as well?"

"Who would train me?" she asked. There was a wealth of sadness blended with resignation in the simple question. In sudden insight, he realized this beautiful, quiet woman was most likely the only one of her kind, totally alone, isolated by necessity.

"Do you mind if I ask some questions?" he gently asked her.

"I understand it is necessary I tell you whatever you need to know in order for us to work together efficiently," Talia hedged.

She didn't really answer his question, but he let it go.

"You were able to contact my brother through me from half a world away."

"Yes."

"So why is it necessary to take you on location?"

"I can contact him, but I can't track him from that distance. Also, the other Seals may be in equally rough shape in this

26

situation. Without a link, I need to be in physical proximity in order to assess and stabilize them."

"Why?"

"I need to be in a person's auric field in order to read them accurately."

"Are you in my field?"

"Yes."

"What do you read about me?"

"Enough that I have what I need to know. I try to avoid gaining information about anyone unless it is absolutely necessary to obtain it. I will afford you your privacy the best I am able."

"So go ahead and read me," he offered.

"Are you testing me? Do you wonder what I can see, or if I can see at all?" she asked, looking up into his face with her piercing gray eyes.

"Maybe," he admitted, meeting her stare.

"It is not wise to play with that kind of fire, Agent Pane," she said, returning her attention to the window.

Gooseflesh rose on his arms. What was it about this woman?

"What happened to you in the lab last night?"

"Exactly what are you referring to?"

"All of it, but let's start with the bruises and internal injuries."

"Your brother had been badly beaten. His ribs had been broken, and one punctured his right lung. He was drowning on his own blood." She felt the big man flinch and knew it was painful to hear of his brother's suffering.

"Somehow you were able to take that on?"

"Yes, in order to heal him directly I need to be able to be in his field. That was not an option last night. He was dying, so I absorbed the injuries into my own body from where I could heal them."

"And you were able to save Daniel by taking on his injuries?"

"Yes."

"Did you feel his pain?" Nickolas wanted to know.

"Yes," she answered simply.

"Thank you," he said softly, deeply moved by her willingness to suffer in order to save his brother. Talia shrugged and looked back out the window.

"In my orders, it states I am to be the only one to touch you. Why is that?"

"Damage control."

"What do you mean?"

She silently looked into his face for so long, he was sure she wasn't going to answer.

"You have been touched by me, agent, what do you think?" she finally asked in challenge.

His cock nearly jumped out of his pants, clearly stating *its* thoughts on the matter.

"Do you have that effect on everyone?" he asked, though it was admitting she had gotten to him.

"So far, yes."

"Men and women alike?"

"Yes."

"Straight or gay?"

"Both."

Holy shit!

"Indeed."

He knew he had not spoken the explicative out loud. He also knew she had responded to it as if he had. She was back to looking out the window. He took the opportunity to regroup.

Once again, this tiny woman had shaken the Ice Man. He had never been thrown so far off balance in his entire life. He wanted to run as far from her as fast as he could, and at the same time he wanted to possess her and never let her out of his sight. He wanted so deep inside her, she would never be free of him.

"Dear god, woman, what are you?" he asked without meaning to.

"No one knows," she whispered.

They silently looked at each other.

"I am sorry, you know," she said.

"Sorry about what?"

"I have read you enough to know you're a good man, Agent Pane. You deserve better than what this will do to you, what I will do to you. Please understand, there are more than twenty of them. I cannot, will not turn my back on those young men, your brother included."

"Nor will I," he assured her.

Over the cabin speaker, he heard the pilot announcing their descent to Charlotte where they would have an hour and a half layover before their next flight. As they disembarked, they were met by a female airport security agent that offered to escort Talia to the ladies room. Though he knew to expect her, Nickolas asked for her ID, which she willingly produced. He stood outside the restroom door for a surprisingly short time before the agent and Talia reemerged.

"Would you like some coffee?" Agent Miller offered after escorting them to a private lounge. "You will be boarding your flight to New York in about an hour."

Both Talia and Nickolas accepted her offer, and shortly thereafter, coffee was delivered, accompanied by croissants and jam. Nickolas noticed Talia sipped her coffee but didn't eat.

"Were you debriefed on our itinerary?" he asked.

"No."

That there had not been time to debrief her was not surprising, given what she had gone through the night before. What had him baffled was her apparent lack of interest. Leaving all the arrangements to him, she had followed his instructions without asking a single question.

"We will arrive in New York in time for a late lunch. We have been booked at the W Hotel for the night. Our new identities will be assumed there, and we can rest up before starting the overseas portion of our trip in the morning," he informed her. She nodded.

"You don't seem to have much interest."

"I trust you to see to the details of the trip, Agent Pane."

"I appreciate that, but I would have thought you might at least want to know what to expect from one day to the next."

"Being in public requires my full attention. It's about all I can manage right now," she said, smiling mysteriously.

"You're going to have to explain that one to me." He knew he should let it drop, but he really needed to understand this woman he was responsible for. It was professional interest only. He was not becoming obsessed, he assured himself. It was necessary to know what made her tick in order to protect her. That he also needed to know all he could about her for his own peace of mind, he chose to ignore. Just then, another couple entered the lounge.

"She is not his wife but his mistress. They are on their way to Vegas. He paid extra for the private lounge to not be seen with her more than necessary. He is relatively sure his wife is on to him and has hired a PI. His head is full of what they will do in bed when they get to their room in Caesar's Palace. She is thinking about what shows they will catch and what all she can rook him into buying for her. She plans to start her shopping trip at Christian Dior. Her feet hurt and she will probably kick off her heels as soon as she sits down. His prostate is giving him grief, so he won't sit but go straight to the bathroom. When he comes back, he plans to swing by the bar and get them each a martini. While he is gone, she intends to look you over more thoroughly."

Nickolas looked at Talia questioningly, then observed the couple that had just come in. The man was in his mid-fifties to early sixties, well dressed and clearly loaded, judging by his suit, watch and horse-turd sized diamond pinky ring. The arm candy was at least thirty years younger than he, dressed in a black lace camisole and red leather suit, with a short skirt and matching three inch heels. Her thick brown hair was highlighted in blonde and red streaks and swept up in a cascade of curls, probably polyester, that hung down her back. When they reached a table across the room, the older man helped her to a seat before turning to go to the men's restroom. She kicked off her heels, ran one stockinged foot up the calf of her other leg, looked Nickolas up and down, and licked her red lips provocatively while staring into his eyes.

Nickolas looked back at Talia in amazement.

"Sort of gives TMI a whole new meaning, doesn't it?" she added with a small, tight smile.

Nickolas looked back at the couple's table to see the man return with two martinis, and shook his head in disbelief.

"So you have to concentrate in order to get all that intel? That's why you're distracted?" he asked her.

"No, I have to concentrate in order *not* to get all that intel, as you call it," she corrected. "If I relax for even a moment, I get all of that, times the number of people in the room."

Holy shit!

"Exactly, if you drop the 'holy,'" she said to his unspoken response.

"So, fool that I am, I just have to ask, is there anything you don't know about me at this point?" Nickolas inquired, feeling strangely exposed.

"I only know that, for the most part, I can trust you and the basic caliber of your character. You're much more contained, not leaky like most people, so I find it much easier to afford you your privacy."

"But you could read me if you chose?"

"Maybe not, particularly now that you know it's something I do."

"What do you mean?"

"You, sir, are not without your own gifts," she said cryptically. "You are naturally able to block your thoughts. I find you restful to be around."

~ CHAPTER SIX ~

Airborne Navy Seal, Lieutenant Commander Daniel Pane was in a world of hurt. He and thirty other Seals had jumped into Iraq on a rescue mission, only to find they had been set up. There was no other way they could have been taken so efficiently, or so quickly. Even though it had been a night jump, a third of the men never made it to the ground alive. When enemy fire opened up, they were sitting (or floating) ducks hanging from chutes. It was just a matter of dumb luck that he made it down alive. Not that he considered being a POW lucky in the least.

Now he was a reluctant "guest" of a cell of the Taliban. Hell, they had not even been sure the bastards were responsible for the first capture of Seals a week before. Well, he was sure now. His command of Arabic was good enough to pick that up, though he would be damned if he let the fucking rag-heads know he understood them.

They had been beaten, bound, gagged, and thrown into the canvas covered beds of three domestic trucks, then taken to different locations. He and seven other Seals had ended up here, wherever here was. He had been singled out and separated from the rest, probably due to his rank. They had worked him over for several days trying to get information, but he hadn't broken.

There had been a point when he knew he was dead – then, the angel dream. Though he thought of it as a dream, he knew it to be much more. She had somehow healed his internal injuries, saving his life. He couldn't remember most of what she'd said as he'd been at death's door, but several things were clear. She was with his brother Nickolas, and they were looking for him. When she pulled away from him, she said something else he remembered.

"I've healed you inside, but left enough evidence of your injuries on the outside so they won't know. Play possum. Let them think you are still near death. We'll find you, just hang on." Her soft voice had been strained as if she were in pain, then she was gone.

Well, he was hanging, but he didn't know how much longer he could manage. He knew some of the other Seals were in close proximity since he could hear beatings and screams of agony. He was locked alone in a windowless hovel with a dirt floor and nothing else, wallowing in his own filth.

Occasionally, two or three of them would come in and pour brackish water down his throat, kick him a couple of times, ask him, in thickly accented English, if he was ready to talk or if they had to dismember another of his men, then leave him alone in the darkness. That appeared to be their new tactic. Thinking he was too near death to survive another beating himself, they isolated him in the dark and let him hear the suffering of his men. He would rather take another beating. The bastards probably knew that.

Another agonized set of screams broke the air and he cringed. Crap, if he weren't so fucking dehydrated, he would probably have pissed himself. This was the worst yet, the scream seeming to go on forever. Suddenly the door opened and something was thrown inside, landing up against his face where it rested on the dirt floor. They left the door open long enough to be sure he had enough light to recognize the disembodied left hand still wearing its wedding band, then shut it, laughing among themselves. Bound as he was, all he could do was lay face down while the warmth left the severed appendage and he felt the chill enter the limp fingers where they rested against his cheek.

36

~ CHAPTER SEVEN ~

During the smooth and uneventful flight from Charlotte, Talia had been still and quiet looking out of the window. After a hair-raising ride, the limo that picked them up at the airport stopped, thankfully, in front of the W Hotel on Times Square. A footman all but jerked open her door while a bellboy rushed out to load their luggage onto a cart, accompanied by honks and curses from cars whizzing by on the busy street.

The ground level entry was unremarkable, leading to an elevator that took them to the fourth floor where the lobby was located. Nickolas made short work of checking them in, mindful of the full bar just across the elegant windowless room. Even though it was only around noon, cocktails and conversations were flowing. He was sure it was a less than ideal environment for the sensitive Miss Martin. She stood to one side, close to their cart, subtly using it as a buffer between her and passersby.

The lobby, with its open bar, had been bad enough, but the elevator was an exercise in torture. Agent Pane, bless him, had positioned her in a corner, placing himself and the luggage cart between her and the rest of the crowd that loaded on after them. With the huge bank of elevators, why everyone thought they just *had* to get on the one she was in was beyond her. Tired as she was, she almost would have preferred flying straight through rather than spending the night in, of all places, Times Square. For pity's sake, could whatever pinhead that had arranged their itinerary have found anyplace more crowded?

She hated everything about New York. From the rude, frantic pace of the traffic and the way she had been rushed out of the limo, to the self-absorbed, vain, overdressed patrons of the neon and chrome bar, the place was cold, unfriendly, and downright gaudy. Gad, what she wouldn't give to be back in her little house with a cat on her lap.

The elevator doors slid open on the fourteenth floor, and they were forced to push their way past the elevator full of prattling cattle. Agent Pane did his best to shield her, but as fate would have it, a man lifted his arm to groom his fashion-plate hair just as she was trying to get past him. His hand made contact with her bare arm. For one split second, they both froze. She looked at the floor and tried to get past, but he reflexively grabbed her arm and pulled her toward him.

Shit.

She tugged, trying to get away without a scene, but it was not to be.

"Not so fast, princess, where are you going? What's your room number?" he whispered huskily in her ear.

Suddenly, a large fist closed around the man's wrist and began to apply pressure.

"I strongly suggest you unhand my wife," Agent Pane softly instructed.

"She was coming on to me," the jackass had the gall to whine after releasing Talia's arm. "I have every right to expect her to deliver." As he rubbed his abused wrist, the other people in the elevator started bitching about the delay. God forbid, thirty seconds stolen from their busy, ever so important lives.

"Get out of our way, or I will be the one to deliver," Pane hissed at him. The man paled and wisely stepped aside.

"What did you see in that little frump anyway, Carl?" a woman's voice demanded as the elevator door slid shut on the laughing cosmopolitans, leaving Talia and Nickolas blessedly alone on their floor. Talia continued to look down, not meeting his eyes. He could see she was pale and shaken, her cheeks flaming in her white face, shame rolling off of her in waves.

"You did nothing to deserve that, and you are the furthest thing from a frump I have ever seen," he assured her. She responded with a single shake of her head, still not looking up.

"Come on, let's get into our room," he said, moving the cart forward and reaching for her arm to escort her.

She jumped back from him as if a snake had struck.

"Sorry, I forgot," he apologized, then waited for her to head down the hall in front of him where he could keep an eye on her. "Looks like it's the one on the left at the end of the hall."

The room was a study in monochrome grays and soft lighting. A fuchsia throw on the foot of the bed, matching pillow on the leather chaise lounge, and flowers in a clear vase provided the only color. The door closed behind them, shutting off all sound from the hall. After all the flash, neon and glitz, Talia found it strangely restful. Then she noticed the king sized bed.

"Not to worry, there is an adjoining room," Nickolas informed her with a little smile, having noticed her eyeing the bed. "For appearances, we will come and go from this room as a couple," he said as he inspected the bathroom, and opened the door to the adjoining room. An identical, but mirror image, room waited on the other side. There were new suitcases on luggage racks in both rooms.

Nickolas went in ahead of her, giving the room and the bath a thorough search before indicating she could enter.

"If you would like, go ahead and freshen up, I'll meet you in here when you're done," he said, indicating the first room they had entered. She nodded and waited for him to close the adjoining door. He didn't. Instead, he stood there looking down at her intently.

"You Okay?" he finally asked. She hadn't spoken one word since their debarkation at JFK. He figured it was because she was "concentrating," but the incident in the elevator had clearly shaken her.

"Pedophile," she blurted, then regretted it immediately.

"I beg your pardon?" Nickolas couldn't have been more taken aback.

"That man, the one on the elevator, he molests children." No help for it now that she'd let the cat out of the bag, she needed to clarify lest Agent Pane thought she was referring to him.

Nickolas braced himself against what the contact would do to him before putting one large forefinger under her chin. He forced her face up until her eyes meet his. Her skin was velvet under his finger, stormy gray eyes searching his. Barely banked lust rushed to the forefront, but he managed to hold it in check – just.

"You did nothing to deserve the way that jerk treated you, and there is nothing you can do about what he is," he assured her. "Just because you are privy to information doesn't make it your responsibility."

How had he known? This enigma of a man, giant, hard and uncompromising, was sensitive enough to understand her pain and try to ease it. He even touched her without bleeding his feelings into her or succumbing to lust. It felt so good to be touched. Just his strong, warm finger under her chin was a balm to her, a momentary relief from her agonizing, life-long, total isolation.

~ CHAPTER EIGHT ~

"Come on in," he invited when she knocked at the adjoining door. She stepped through, and his heart stopped. Damn, but she was a beauty. She had changed out of the linen travel suit and now wore a steely-blue silk wrap-around dress. It had a deep "v" neckline where the fabric crossed over her full breasts, and tied at one hip. The skirt flared out soft and sassy, ending just above her knees. Her petite feet were encased in strappy navy heeled sandals. *Yum!* It was all he could do not to walk over to her, untie her sash and let her hair out of that damned French roll.

"I didn't think you would be overly anxious to go back out into the jungle, so I had lunch delivered." He indicated the tray of finger sandwiches on the mirrored gray counter along one wall. She crossed the room and sat on the desk chair at the counter, picked up a dainty cocktail napkin and a small sandwich. She crossed one long shapely leg over the other and her dress opened slightly, exposing a creamy thigh. *Double yum!*

"You should be sainted," she said, closing her eyes in pure culinary enjoyment over the simple offering.

"Hardly," he responded, trying not to stare at her exposed thigh. God, this entire assignment was going to be one damned exercise in torture, he surmised, as his pants became increasingly uncomfortable.

After she had eaten her fill, she noticed several objects he'd laid out on the counter next to the tray of sandwiches. Among them were passports, driver's licenses, shot cards, credit cards, an assortment of tickets, and two small white jewelry boxes.

"Our new identities," he informed her, when he saw she was looking at the substantial pile. "For the next leg of our trip, we will be traveling as Mr. and Mrs. Wade Sinclair. Your first name is Julianne. Jewel for short." He reached over, picked up one of the boxes and opened it. Nestled in white velvet was a yellow gold engagement ring set with a huge brilliant cut diamond. It was paired with a matching diamond studded wedding band.

"Your rings, my dear," he said, offering the box up in a humorous flourish. He took them out, surprising her by taking her left hand.

He realized he was beginning to actually look forward to the powerful rush that ran through his body every time he touched her. He took her hand and slid the wedding band, then the engagement ring, onto her ring finger. As the predictable lust slammed into his gut at the contact, he also recognized it felt good to lay claim to her, even in this small way.

He took up the other box, and put the matching gold and diamond man's wedding band on his left ring finger. Yes, he liked the look of the matched set on their hands. The constant overload of testosterone must be melting his brain, he concluded.

"I'm an engineering consultant for Saudi Aramco Oil Company. Do I look the part?" he said, arching one eyebrow, attempting to look debonair and drawing a girlish giggle from Talia. The sound of her mirth caressed his cock with invisible fingers. It had a sobering effect. There was only so much a man could take.

"I'm sorry; it's just that you look more like a kick-butt SS agent than a wimpy consultant," she apologized, misunderstanding the cause for his sudden change in demeanor.

"What? Is my shoulder holster showing?" he joked, looking down at his black suit jacket in mock concern, trying to put her at ease.

"No, I think it is your attitude peeking through," she smiled back.

He liked this side of her. Her amazing eyes sparkling and full lips tipping up in humor added to an already breathtaking beauty. Yes, fool that he was, he liked this side of her, but probably wasn't going to survive it.

~ CHAPTER NINE ~

Daniel had begun to doubt his sanity. Sometimes, when he drifted off, he could swear he felt the angel's soft fingers on his face, soothing and healing, then he would snap awake and realize he had come up against the hand of his buddy. Rigor mortis had set in, the hand now cold and stiff next to his face. He'd recognized that shiny new wedding band, had held it in his pocket at Sam's wedding when he stood up with him. Sam had been so damn proud of that ring, and Gloria, his beautiful new wife.

They thought the hand would break him? Dumb fucks. It only made him more determined to live. He would get that ring back to Gloria or die trying. God willing, he would find Sam alive and bring him back as well, but he'd be damned if he let them break him. Now they had *really* pissed him off. Every time he opened his eyes and saw that hand, a cold killing rage burned deeper in his gut. If anyone could find them, Nickolas would, and he would have his revenge. He, by god, lived for it.

~ CHAPTER TEN ~

They spent the afternoon in Nickolas' room going over the mission, their itinerary and the details of their cover. At first blush, the mission was fairly simple – slip into Iraq via Saudi Arabia, locate his brother and the other Seals using Talia's unique skills, then relay that location to the multiple special ops teams on standby and get the hell out of Dodge. As usual, the devil was in the details, Nickolas thought to himself. He hated putting her at risk. She was small, delicate and civilian. He had no idea how she would respond under fire. That there would be fire of some sort was a given on any mission like this, no matter how careful the planning. He also realized that, without her, the chances of finding his brother alive were next to nil. She'd already saved his life once, Nickolas reminded himself.

Thankfully, there were two other sets of military/SS personnel traveling undercover with them. Dr. Wilkinson, who had apparently done so with Talia before, and an Army medic, Franklin, were posing as father and son on a Middle Eastern vacation. Their presence was a great relief to Nickolas, given Talia's propensity to take on other people's injuries. Agents Samuels and Carlton from the SS would also be shadowing them from New York. Nickolas was their superior and had worked with the two very capable agents. They were booked on the same flights and hotels, providing more backup. Both men were dark and could pass for Arab, undercover as merchants on a buying trip. It was a minimal team, but all they dared if they were to remain undetected.

It was dinner time when they finally finished going over the debriefing.

"You hungry?" he asked her as he stood and stretched.

"Getting there, are you?"

"Yeah, getting there myself. Why don't you go change into evening wear? We have reservations at Smith & Wollensky's in about an hour. Ever been there?"

"No."

"Their food is pretty good and the environment quiet. I think you'll like it," he paused, "if you're carnivorous, that is." Nickolas looked at her questioningly.

"Carnivorous, yes, I can do carnivorous," she assured him with an anticipatory smile.

~

When she returned to his room, she was a knockout in the proverbial little black dress and strappy high heels. Good god, who did her wardrobe? He didn't know if they should be shot or commended, maybe both.

"Who arranges for your clothes?" he had to ask.

"I'm not sure; they just always do it when I'm on assignment. I don't think they trust me to dress according to cover. Why, is there something wrong?" she said in concern, looking down at her short, low cut, form-fitting, spandex, little nothing of a dress. He groaned, shaking his head.

"No, it's perfect, absolutely appropriate to our cover and the occasion," he assured her. "The problem is how you look in it," the devil in him added.

"How do I look in it?" she asked, now really becoming concerned. "Am I too heavy for it?"

"God, no, woman, the way you look in it, it'll take my entire team to keep men off of you."

"It's the one they had marked for tonight, should I change?"

"No, I will endeavor to endure," he said with a self-deprecating smile as he held out his arm, inviting her to lace hers through it. She looked at his offered arm, then up at him, hesitating. "What the hell. Might as well go for broke; you and that dress have already brought me to my knees. Besides, I want it perfectly clear who you're with. No more mistakes like the one on the elevator, or I may have to kill someone."

When they reached the ground level entry, Nickolas could tell she recognized Agent Samuels as he got into a cab with another large, equally dark man. To her credit, she made no indication that she even saw, much less knew him. The doorman hailed them their own cab, and Nickolas helped her in, sliding in beside her.

He looked down on the top of her well coiffured head, impressed with her composure. He had not seen her make one mistake the entire trip. Again, he wondered at her level of training. It was a conversation they would have to have soon. He really needed to have some idea of what to expect from her. He found his mind wandering to what he would *like* to be able to expect from her, before he managed to rein in his thoughts and pay attention to their arrival at the restaurant. The cab pulled to a sudden, jarring stop under the awning of a classic black and white corner building. "Smith & Wollensky Steaks and Chops" was written in bold white letters on a black background around the top of the building.

When they walked inside, they were greeted with a rich combination of dark hardwood wainscoting, oak floors, beige walls and massive skylights. Black, wooden ladder-back chairs with tan cushions were set around white clothed tables. The dark hardwood bar sported an impressive selection of wines in racks that reached the ceiling. The atmosphere was open and airy, managing to blend casual comfort with formal grace.

Nickolas braced himself, and took her arm to escort her behind the maître d' who, as chance would have it, seated them in the same room with the other two agents. As they entered the room to the click of her high heels on the wood floor, heads turned, and numerous sets of male eyes appreciatively locked onto the woman next to him – every set of male eyes in the place, to be exact. Agent Samuels, somewhat prepared from having seen her before, managed not to drool, but poor Carlton nearly swallowed his tongue before pulling himself together.

Unwarranted pride filled Nickolas' chest. He was just her bodyguard, and she wasn't really his wife, but the feel of her soft arm in his hand stirred something new he wasn't overly willing to inspect. Any man would be proud to be seen with this woman, he told himself, brushing the unfamiliar feelings off with the thought.

After he seated her and took his own chair, Talia looked at the arrestingly handsome agent from under her lashes. As usual, he was dressed in a dark suit, charcoal this time with a dove gray shirt and dark gray tie. His electric blue eyes took in their environment with seemingly casual regard, but she was sure he didn't miss a thing. In one ear, he had what appeared to be a very small hearing aid she assumed was a com device, as was the small diamond pin on his lapel. His willingness to touch her often had her off balance. The feel of his large, warm palm at the small of her back, or on her elbow as he escorted her, was both provocative and arousing. The way he towered over her, his tall solid frame shielding her, was more comforting than threatening. That, too, was a novel experience, but the lack of mental bombardment was the most remarkable. For the first time in her life, she had no idea what the person beside her was thinking or feeling. She found that, and him, extremely intriguing, not to mention sexy as all get out.

"Would you like some wine?" he asked, drawing her from her thoughts.

"Yes, that sounds lovely."

"Is red and dry Okay?"

"Perfect."

He ordered a bottle of Louis Jadot Beaujolais and lobster cocktails. When the waiter delivered them, she found them both delicious. They enjoyed the wine and appetizers in companionable silence as they perused the menus.

"Do you know what you want, or would you like me to order for you?" he asked, as he noticed the waiter heading their way again.

"You've done great so far, I think I'll have you do it, if you don't mind," she answered, grateful to have him take over the task. As usual, she was distracted, fielding all the mental chatter and feelings in the crowded room.

"How do you like your steak?"

"Medium rare."

He ordered her the Filet Oscar, the Cajun Spiced Filet Mignon for himself, both medium rare, and a Caesar salad for each of them.

"So, what do you do when you're not traveling the world playing Florence Nightingale?" he asked. She looked up at him sharply to discern if he was being sarcastic, and decided he was just making polite, safe conversation. In a public place, it would not do to ask what she did when she was not undercover for the government.

"Graphic design. I work online out of my home," she responded honestly.

"What sort of design?"

"Oh, a little of a lot of things, book covers and illustrations mostly. How about you, are you always someone's hero?" she asked, trying to shift the attention from her isolated, pathetic life. It was his turn to look into her face for sarcasm. Seeing none, he decided to be honest as well.

"I only do this part time any more. I'm called in on special assignments."

"What do you do with yourself on your off time?"

"Believe it or not, I'm a rancher."

"A rancher?"

"Yes, I semi-retired to take over the family ranch when my father and mother were killed five years ago."

"I'm so sorry, about your folks I mean. How were they killed?"

"Car accident. How about your folks? Are they still alive?" She looked down at her wine glass and twirled it around slowly by the stem, remaining silent for so long he was sure she wouldn't answer.

"I never knew who they were," she finally said.

"How so?" He was intrigued.

"I was dropped off in the waiting room of a police station when I was a couple months old. No one saw who did it."

"What about your adoptive parents?"

"I guess I cried a lot; the state even had trouble placing me in foster care. Eventually, they misdiagnosed me with autism, so I grew up first in an orphanage, then an institution. I obtained my degree in graphic design online through vocational rehab, got my house through Habitat for Humanity, and there you have my exciting life."

"How did you end up doing this?" She knew "this" meant working for the government.

"When I was in my teens living in the institution, one of the aides there took me under her wing. She was a sweet lady in her fifties and smarter than most, I guess. Anyway, she was into psychic phenomena and had somehow put it together that I was psychic, not autistic. One day when she came into work, she was really upset. I 'heard' her worrying about her nephew and his wife. Her nephew was a private pilot and had not closed his flight plan. Later that day she was called into the office. Her brother, a major in the army, had come to let her know his son was missing and assumed down. I liked her and really felt sorry for her. She had often spoken of her nephew and how proud she was of him. I stood by the office door, and when the two of them walked out, I looked her in the eye and told her I could probably help."

"And she believed you?"

"Well, I kind of made an impression, because she had never heard me speak before."

"You didn't talk?"

"No, not really."

"Why?"

"I already knew more about most people than I wanted, and I just got tired of being lied to."

"So what happened?"

"We all went back into the office, and she sat me down with her brother. He was skeptical, but when I told him what he was thinking, it set him back." How well Talia could remember the look on the older man's face when she told him he was already thinking about having to bury his son next to his wife who had died of breast cancer two years earlier. When she described the dead woman's unusual tombstone, a full sized, pink marble statue of the Virgin Mary, she had his full attention.

"Anyway, when I put my finger on his wrist I 'saw' his son and daughter-in-law on a mountainside in a Cessna that had crashed. She was dead, and he was trapped in the wreckage. I guess I blurted out what I saw as well as his son's name. He used his rank and pulled strings in order to check me out of the institution, and managed to get us both on a search and rescue helicopter. We found his son in time to save him. Fortunately, the major was a good man, and never acted upon the impulses toward me that he was left with after working with me.

Unfortunately, he never got beyond it, and he shot himself a year later. Apparently, though, no good deed goes unpunished. After rescuing his son, rather than take me back to the institution as he had promised, the major shared the information of what I'd done with his friend in special ops. The major had me do several demos for his friend who immediately arranged to have me housed and trained. They put me on difficult situations like this one. After several successful missions, they arranged for me to get my education and home, but they always keep an eye on me. I'm still pulled in from time to time, and the rest you know."

"I'm amazed they didn't try to enlist you."

"Oh, they did. In fact, they sort of commandeered me into special ops whether I wanted to be or not, but I don't play well with others."

"How so?"

"It's too difficult for me to be around people. When Dr. Wilkinson assured them to do so would burn me out and render me useless to them, they set me up with my own place using Habitat as a cover. How about you, how did you get into what you do?" she shifted the conversation.

"I have always been an idealistic, protective SOB, and I wanted to make a difference. It just sort of evolved naturally for me," he shared, realizing she was growing increasingly uncomfortable discussing her past.

"But you retired," she pointed out.

"Yeah, I was the only one with the skills to take over the ranch. Besides, I discovered that most people I was assigned to protect weren't worth protecting," he confessed.

"Like me?"

"No, Talia, not like you." It was the first time he had called her by her first name.

"You consider me worth protecting?"

"I do, absolutely, yes."

Their dinner arrived and conversation shifted to the mundane. Nickolas couldn't help but marvel over what he had learned about the woman in his care. Now, realizing she had been discovered by a major in the Army, his having been sent to Fort Stewart, an Army installation instead of Navy, made more sense. He was amazed at how well adapted she seemed after her horrific upbringing. She had said more tonight – shared more than during rest of their combined time together. Her quiet demeanor made a lot more sense to him now, as did her intriguing combination of classy refinement and naiveté. He'd also found out she had some special ops training, for which he was eternally grateful. How extensive that training had been, he still had no idea, but any was better than none at all.

"Would you like some dessert?" he asked when they had finished their meal.

"Oh, no thank you, I couldn't eat another bite. Though I don't mind waiting if you want some," she assured him.

"No, I'm not much into sweets. You ready to go?"

"Yes, if you are."

"Samuels, we're about out of here," he spoke softly after touching his lapel, confirming her suspicions about his com equipment.

After paying the tab with an American Express in their cover name, he stood, walked around the table and pulled out her chair. When she preceded him out of the room, and he put his palm on the small of her back, he could swear he felt her shudder.

"Does it bother you when I touch you?" he asked, leaning down to one of her shell-like ears. He saw gooseflesh rise up her bare arm at his whispered question.

"No, not exactly, doesn't it bother you?" she asked.

"Everything about you bothers me, lady," he replied, not removing his hand. Instead, he used his long fingers on her small waist to draw her closer to him.

He was just keeping up appearances for their cover, she decided, and went with him willingly. He hailed a cab out front and slid into the seat beside her. After instructing the driver to return them to the hotel, he looked down at her with unreadable electric blue eyes, but said nothing. She suddenly felt like a rabbit in a snare.

"What?" she asked, unable to endure his scrutiny any longer.

"You are probably the most beautiful woman I have ever seen."

"You probably should not be touching me so much," she advised.

"I thought you were the most beautiful woman I had seen before you touched me, Talia, and for the record, I wanted you from the first moment I saw you."

"Why are you telling me this?" His words shook her deeply, in a delicious, arousing sort of way.

"You said you can't read me, is that right?"

"For the most part, yes, that's true."

"I just thought you should know," he said softly as he ran the backs of his fingers down her bare arm, then laced them with her hand in her lap. He lifted her hand to his mouth and ran his warm, full lips over her knuckles as he looked into her eyes.

Talia almost jumped out of her skin when the doorman at the W snatched their cab door open. Nickolas handed the driver some bills, got out, offered her his hand and drew her out of the cab and under his arm.

"A little jumpy?" he asked with a smile.

"I sometimes get that way when I'm over tired."

"As in being around too many people for too long?"

"Yes, exactly."

"I won't let anything happen to you, Talia," he whispered the promise into her ear to prevent anyone hearing him address her by her real name. She shivered before looking up at him searchingly.

"I know you'll do your best," she said. He could not help but feel there was hidden meaning to her words.

When they reached their rooms he preceded her in, drew his Beretta and went through his room and bath. Then he pulled her into his room, closed the door and left her standing there in order to search her room as well.

"I would know," she told him.

"Know what?" he asked as he rejoined her.

"If there were someone waiting in here for us, I would know."

"Would you know if I were in here?"

"Oh, yes," she answered emphatically.

"How would you know if you can't read me?"

"I feel you," she responded, raising his blood pressure by several points.

"Feel me?"

"Yes."

"How do I feel?" he asked as he stepped closer to her. He knew he was crowding her, but couldn't seem to help himself. She surprised him by not retreating.

"Warm, large, solid, grounded and very male. You also feel like you could be dangerous under the right circumstances," she said, after standing still with her eyes closed as if to take him in. He could tell she wasn't trying to be provocative, but rather just answering his question.

"What circumstances?"

"If I were your enemy."

"And if you aren't my enemy? You aren't, are you, little Talia?" he asked, reaching up to run the backs of his fingers down her velvet cheek.

"No, I'm not your enemy."

"Then am I dangerous to you?" She looked into his eyes for the longest time before she slowly nodded.

"Yes, I think you can be very dangerous to me."

"Yet, you trust me?"

"Yes."

"Maybe you shouldn't."

"Why?"

"I'm going to kiss you unless you tell me you don't want me to," he declared as he wrapped his hand around her nape and slowly pulled her to him. He searched her eyes, giving her plenty of time to protest, but she said nothing. She watched him with wide, liquid gray eyes as he lowered his mouth to hers and gently brushed her lips with his.

He could have sworn he was at ground zero of the Twin Towers as his entire being imploded. Fool that he was, he had to taste her, regardless. He opened his mouth over hers and ran his tongue along the seam of her lips, but she didn't open for him, so he slowly pulled back and put his forehead against hers.

"I'm sorry; I had no right to do that," he said, releasing her and stepping away. She continued to watch him with those cool gray eyes, saying nothing. God, she had rocked his world, and she stood there without a hair out of place. "I suppose we should call it a night, our flight leaves at 11:20 tomorrow morning. We'll need to eat breakfast before we leave. The limo will pick us up at 08:30."

"Good night, Agent Pane," she said, and went into her room, softly closing the door.

~ CHAPTER ELEVEN ~

"And if you are not my enemy? You're not, are you, little Talia?" He could almost feel the backs of his fingers as they ran down her velvet cheek.

Daniel snapped awake at the sound of Nickolas' voice. He could have sworn his brother was in the room with him – no, not in the hovel, more like in another room, one full of soft light and a beautiful woman. He could almost catch her scent. Talia, Nickolas had called her Talia; it had to be the angel in his dream. Was she an enemy? God, he wished he could clear his head, but dehydration and the repeated physical trauma were taking their toll.

Enemy or not, he could tell his hardnosed, shut down brother had feelings for this woman. It was there in his voice. Nickolas had not been the same after his wife betrayed him. Nancy had been beautiful, too – but cold, spoiled and self indulgent to the extreme. When the death of their parents had necessitated Nickolas taking over the ranch, Nancy had flat refused to live in the country. She insisted Nickolas set her up in a town home where she proceeded to go on shopping sprees and entertain lovers.

At first, Nickolas was so overwhelmed with grieving his parents and running the ranch, he didn't catch on. He'd driven six hours on their fourth anniversary to surprise her, only to discover she was not alone.

Daniel never knew all the details, but his brother had not been the same after that. To his knowledge, Nickolas had never become close to another woman in the five years after his divorce. In all that time, Daniel had never heard his brother speak to a woman like he was just talking to Talia. If indeed it was Nickolas and not a damned hallucination, he thought wryly, drifting back into unconsciousness.

~ Chapter Twelve ~

Not long after Talia had gone to her room, Nickolas was sitting sideways on the chaise, cleaning his Beretta, when he heard a loud thump and a whimper of pain coming from behind her closed door. He had the clip back in the hand gun, a bullet in the chamber, and was across the room before the sound faded from the air. Gun pointing upward and held in a two handed grip, he kicked her door open and crouched into her room from around the door jamb at full draw, scanning the area for any threat.

She was across the room looking at him in shock, absently rubbing her creamy thigh where she had run into the nightstand on her way to bed. Soft light came in through the bathroom door, illuminating her petite, shapely form. She was wearing a short nighty in pink satin. It barely covered her curvaceous ass and was cut low and sexy, accentuating her full breasts. He could see her pert little nipples rising under the sheer fabric. Did that mean she wanted him? God, he hoped so. He lived in a constant state of painful arousal; the least she could do was want him a little.

"It's Okay, I just ran into the table," she said, indicating one long shapely leg. He stood and holstered his gun, never taking his eyes from her. He was breathing hard, like he had just run a marathon, and his cock strained against his pants. Nickolas inhaled, trying to gather his unraveling control, but her scent filled the room, igniting him further.

"Do you always dress like that for bed?"

"No."

"Then why are you wearing that thing now, to torture me?"

"No."

"Then why?" he demanded in a low voice as he slowly approached her.

"It's what they provided. I usually don't wear anything to bed in the summer, but I thought, because I'm not alone...." He had reached her and stood looking down into her face. He was so close, she could feel the heat radiating from his large body.

"Do you have any idea what that does to a man?"

"What?"

"Hearing that you sleep in the nude."

"No."

"Like hell. I think you enjoy watching me suffer," he accused.

"No."

He reached out, wrapped his long fingered hand around the nape of her neck and pulled her closer. The contact almost brought him to his knees. She didn't pull away, nor did she lean into him. Instead, she watched him closely with those damned cool gray eyes. He was about to incinerate, and she was cool, distant and unaffected. Hell, she didn't even have the sense to be afraid. She needed to be afraid of him. She needed to be terrified of him; god knew, he was scaring himself.

Unable to help it, he lowered his head and took her mouth. Her lips, full, lush and cool, once again remained closed under his. He explored their seam with his tongue, demanding entrance, but they remained closed and unmoving. He wrapped his other arm around her back and pulled her against his hard body, crushing her against his overheated frame, not even trying to hide his enormous throbbing erection, and ground his mouth down on hers. She remained still and seemingly unaffected, not giving in, not pulling away, like he had absolutely no effect on her composure at all.

"Respond to me, damn you." He took her by her upper arms and shook her until her hair fell from its French roll, tumbling across her shoulders and down her back. Her gray eyes were huge, looking into his, but she made no sound. It broke him. He swept her off her feet and threw her on the bed.

In one brutal move, he tore her gown down the front, baring her full, pink tipped breasts. God, they were even more beautiful than he had imagined. She lay perfectly still, looking up at him, making no move to protect or to cover herself.

"God, Talia, tell me to stop now and I'll try to leave you," he all but begged, but she said nothing.

He fell on her, taking one breast into his large hand and covering the nipple of the other with his ravenous, hot mouth. He drew on her as he flicked the nipple of the other breast with his thumb. She shuddered beneath him but didn't fight. Continuing to suckle her breast, he shoved one knee between her legs and drew up the tattered remnants of her gown with his large calloused hand, seeking her core. Dear god, she was wet for him. It was his undoing. He reared back and unzipped his pants; his massive member sprang free, hot and throbbing. He removed the rest of her gown in one savage tear. Throwing it aside he drank in her beauty.

She lay totally still, except for her trembling – an ivory sacrifice. Had the other men she worked with seen her like this? God, he hoped not. The mere thought of it drove him mad. No matter if they had or not, he would make damn sure no one else ever did again. He forced her slender legs apart with bruising force, his powerful fingers sinking into the soft flesh of her thighs, hooked her knees over his forearms and sank into her in a savage thrust. Flesh tore, shocking him as she whimpered in pain, but he couldn't stop. Drawing back, he slammed back into her with all the formidable force of his powerful flanks driving his huge member deep into her quivering depths, drawing another whimper from the beauty, his beauty, by god, HIS. He couldn't stop. Over and over he drove into her with brute force until he roared his orgasm, and it still was not enough.

He ravaged her mouth with his as moans left his throat. He was possessed, his cock still rock hard. He threw her long legs over his shoulders, lifted her hips with both hands and pounded home, roaring orgasm after orgasm, and yet he couldn't stop. His semen mixed with her blood and pooled on the gray bedspread beneath her hips, tears ran down her ivory cheeks, but he could not spare her. God help him, he was going to fuck them both to death. In desperation, he pulled his gun from his holster and shoved it into her tiny hand.

"Stop me. Put the barrel to my god damned head and pull the fucking trigger."

She released the gun, left it lying on the bed next to them and gently laced her trembling arms around his thick neck, holding him tenderly as he continued to pound into her. Finally his entire body seized and arched up as his cock seemed to pierce her very womb. He convulsed repeatedly and then fell on her, spent. He didn't even have the strength to spare her his weight as he crushed her tiny ravaged body beneath him. He was still inside her, swollen and shuddering. She was so tight, he could feel her heartbeat through his cock. Her soft arms were still around his neck, holding him to her tenderly as if he had not just ravaged her, as if he had not just raped her. Even through his lust maddened rampage, he remembered feeling himself tear through her innocence. She had been a virgin, a for-fuck's-sake virgin, and he had just spent the last forty five minutes tearing her apart with his damned over-sized cock.

"Oh, god, Talia, baby, I am so sorry," he groaned in agony.

"I know," she whispered, lacing her fingers in the short hair at his nape in tender, soothing strokes.

"Let me see you," he demanded, pulling away from her to inspect the damage. She flinched in pain as his semi erect member pulled from her, but did not resist. What he saw broke his heart. Long platinum hair flowed around her in tangled disarray. Her lips were swollen and bruised; there were dark fingerprints on her ivory arms and the insides of her soft thighs. More dark prints marred her slender hips where he had cruelly held her for his ravagement. She lay naked in a pool of her own blood, looking up at him with huge, wounded gray eyes. He was fully clothed; his shoes were still on, for fuck's sake. He could see red marks where the rough wool of his pants had chafed her tender skin. His beautiful, proud, contained little treasure lay broken beneath him. She had entrusted him with her protection, and he had savagely and repeatedly raped her for no other reason than she had refused to return his kiss.

"I will send for Dr. Wilkinson and a replacement agent, then I will turn myself in."

"No."

"No? What the fuck do you mean no? We haven't even made it out of New York yet, and I just raped you. You're still bleeding, and I want nothing more than to do it again," he all but roared in her face.

"No, it won't do you any good to turn yourself in. I signed a consent holding you blameless. No, I don't need Wilkinson. As you have seen, I can heal this myself, and no, I don't want another agent, I want you, I want you to hold me until we can do this again. I want you to teach me how to cooperate with you."

"Cooperate?" He was in shock.

"Yes, cooperate; I am sure if you teach me how, I can do it better next time."

"Jesus god, woman!" He sat on the edge of the bed and put his head in his hands, elbows on his knees. "Jesus god," he mumbled from behind his hands. "It was your first time and I was brutal. How can you even bear the thought of my touch?"

"I admit to feeling a little vulnerable right now. I would like for you to hold me if you could bring yourself to do so."

He moaned, turned and lay next to her. He pulled the bedspread around her tiny bruised body and gathered her into his arms. She fit there. She belonged there. In that moment, he knew he could never let her go. He tucked her fair head under his chin and stroked her back to soothe her. God help them both, he could never let her go.

~ CHAPTER THIRTEEN ~

True to her word, her bruises disappeared as she lightly napped in his arms. Her soft breath on his neck had him in an agony of need – his hands shook with it. He had not even managed to get his cock back in his pants, and judging from the rapidly expanding size of it, that was something to be grateful for. He looked down into her perfect face to find her amazing eyes open and watching him.

"If I keep holding you like this, I'm going to end up taking you again," he warned her.

"I know," she whispered, but made no move to leave him.

Cursing, he savagely pushed himself up and away from her. He stomped into the bathroom, painfully shoved himself back into his pants and zipped them up, then wet a wash cloth with warm water and grabbed a hand towel before returning to her. She hadn't moved. She just lay, silent as death, and watched him with seemingly dispassionate eyes.

Cautiously, he pulled back the bedspread. She could see his big hands were shaking. He encouraged her to lie on her back with gentle pressure on her shoulder, and she complied. Her feet were on the bed, knees up and pressed together. He parted them with a warm palm, and carefully cleaned her blood and his seed from her body.

"Am I hurting you?" He had to know. She was so quiet still, giving nothing away.

"No."

"You were a virgin? That was your first time?"

"Yes."

"God, Talia, I am so sorry, you deserved so much better." His deep voice was soft, agonized, and full of regret. She said nothing, watching him in silence. "I would like to be able to promise you it won't happen again, baby, but I won't lie to you. God damn, I'll try, but I can't control myself around you. I don't think I will ever get my fill of you."

"You may."

"Why the hell aren't you running screaming?"

"I won't let this destroy you like it has the others. I won't stand by and watch what I am break you. You are too good a man for that, Nickolas. I just won't do it."

"So you're going to just stick around and let me fuck you to death?" Incredulous anger laced his tone.

"If need be, yes."

"Gods, baby, why?"

"I may not be coming back from this one, Nickolas. I knew it when I took the assignment. I knew it just like when I saw you, I knew I wanted you to be the one."

"The one for what?"

"The one to have me, the one to survive me. I want you to be the one to come back from this, Nickolas. When my nightmare has ended, I want you to be able to live your dreams."

He dropped his head and closed his eyes. She had no way of knowing he had no life, had no dreams. They had all died with his marriage. He had dreamt of a life full of love and laughter, but instead had been used and deceived. He had dreamt of having a family, only to find out his ex had aborted their child rather than risk "ruining her figure." After the way he'd abused Talia, perhaps he had no heart or honor left.

"Look," he said, taking her by the shoulders and capturing her eyes with his intense gaze. "I'll be the first one to admit, I have no idea what you are or how you can do what you do, or the pain you must suffer because of it. I don't begin to understand what you do to me. I have never lost control before. Nothing and no one has been able to break me, and believe me, the best of the best have given it a shot. But you do – without even trying. There is one hell of a lot I don't understand here, but one thing I do know – and hear me well, woman – I will never get my fill of you, I will never let you go, and I will bring you back from this or die trying. We will be walking out of this together or not at all."

"I know you will do your best," she said, and turned her face from him, but not before he saw the tears welling up in her beautiful eyes.

~

"Baby, I can't leave you like this," he whispered, pulling her into his arms.

"Like what?"

"Having been brutalized, I can't have that be the memory of your first time. Will you let me make it right for you?"

"What do you mean?"

"Let me show you what it should be like between a man and a woman."

"I have no skill at all. Is that what you really want to do, or do you just feel sorry for me?" she asked.

"I feel damn sorry I have hurt you, but I want you as well. I will probably always want to make love to you, Talia. I told you I wanted you from the first moment I met you, and I don't see that changing."

"Okay."

"You sure?"

"Yes."

"You scared?"

"Yes."

"Because I hurt you last time?"

"Yes."

God, he wanted to reassure her, but knowing actions speak louder than words, he leaned down and kissed her instead. Her mouth remained closed. This time, however, he recognized it as inexperience, not rejection.

"Have you ever been kissed before?"

"You mean besides you?"

"Yes, besides me."

"Only if you call kicking and scratching while some ass tried to shove his tongue down my throat a kiss."

"Bastard."

"Indeed."

"Who was it?" he demanded in a threatening voice.

"That is classified."

"What do you mean classified?"

"Most every man I worked with was reduced to that at some point or another."

"You didn't kick or scratch me," he had to point out.

"You didn't try to force yourself on me."

"The hell I didn't!"

"No, you didn't. You gave me every chance to say no – first in your room, then in mine."

"Do you think I would have stopped if you had said no?"

"I'm sure of it."

God, he wished he were, he thought, as he lowered his mouth to hers.

"Open your mouth for me, sweetheart," he whispered. He swept his tongue inside when she complied, drawing a shudder from her.

"You Okay?" he asked, pulling back slightly. The last thing he wanted to do was disgust her the way the other men had.

"Umm, yes, Okay, do it again." *Alrighty then* – He gladly complied. Taking his time, he made tender love to her delicious mouth. Her slender arms came up around his neck, and her breathing increased. All good signs, he decided.

"Now put your tongue into my mouth like I did yours," he instructed. She pulled him in closer, crushing his chest to her breasts, and thrust her tongue into his mouth. It took his breath away. Quick study, he observed, as she mimicked his actions. She'd clearly been paying attention. He pulled away and dropped kisses on her neck, then ran his tongue along the pulse point on her throat, obviously an erogenous zone for her, he noted, as she began to squirm. He gently pulled back the covers, exposing her beautiful, full breasts. She blushed but made no move to cover herself. He cupped them in his hands, making an offering of them for himself, and suckled first one, then the other. She was breathing heavily, sinking her hands into his short thick hair to hold him to her.

"Still Okay?" he paused to ask.

"Yes," she almost whimpered, drawing his head back for more. And to think he had taken her to be cold. God, but there was fire in her; he loved it.

"Stay with me here, baby, I'm going to take this to another level," he pleaded in a soothing – if a bit strained – voice as he trailed kisses across her stomach, and took up residence between her legs. She looked down at him questioningly.

"Put those gorgeous legs over my shoulders, like this," he instructed, spreading her wide and putting a leg over each of his broad shoulders. She complied, opening her core to him without protest. God, she was beautiful, her pretty platinum curls wet with rising desire – desire for him; he was her first lover. God, it was a heady thought. He lowered his head to her and ran his tongue over her cleft. She nearly came off the bed. Holy shit, she was responsive. He was still fully clothed and his cock was making a gallant effort at ripping through his suit pants to get at her. Damn, but he wanted in there again. *Soon, buddy, soon, this time is for her.*

He latched onto her clitoris with an openmouthed kiss as he gently penetrated her with one finger. She was tight, clenching around the digit with unbelievable force. He must have torn her apart taking her like he had, he thought with regret, as she literally writhed in his arms. He pulled his finger out before pressing it in deeper while he held her clitoris in his teeth and flicked it with his tongue. He added a second finger, reaching her G spot, and suckled her clit. She came undone for him, crying out in her release and filling his hungry mouth with her sweet cream. He stood and shed his clothes, looking down at her. Holy fuck, she was beautiful in her passion. God, he hoped she was ready for him; he'd never wanted anything like he wanted her right now.

"Will you let me in, baby?" he asked as he rose over her naked, still quaking body. "I promise to try and be gentle this time." She reached up for him in answer, and he covered her soft body with his. Carefully, he guided himself to her wet entrance and slowly started to sink into heaven. She tightened in fear.

"Am I hurting you?" God, don't let him be hurting her, he prayed. She shook her head no.

"Can I come in a little farther?" She nodded.

"You're going to have to relax, baby," he instructed as he pressed forward and she tightened further. Nickolas rolled over onto his back, drawing her with him to sit on top. He pulled her knees up next to his hips, and placed his hands over her full breasts, flicking the nipples with his thumbs.

"There you go, baby, take me as you will. You set the pace."

"But I don't know how," she whispered.

"Here, just sink down on me," he instructed, pulling her down gently with one hand on her hip as he carefully rose up to meet her. She closed her eyes and groaned.

"Did I hurt you?"

"No, it feels so good. It feels so good to have you inside me like this."

"Can you take more of me?"

"I think so."

"Sit down a little more, Oh, god, that's it, baby, take me in," he moaned, throwing his head back in ecstasy as she braced her tiny hands on his chest and sank further onto his torrid cock. She was hot, tight and wet, almost shattering his control. She paused, took a deep breath, then slowly took him to the hilt, settling down until her clit rubbed against his pelvic bone. He shook like a leaf in the wind, clenching and unclenching his fists in the sheets on either side of him to keep from grabbing her hips and pounding into her.

"What do I do now?" she asked.

Reaching between them, he brushed his finger against her erect little nub. She shuddered around him in response.

"Try rubbing this against me," he directed, "See how that feels." Again she followed his instructions exactly, rocking her pelvis back and forth, rubbing her nub against his pubic bone and driving him impossibly deeper. Holy shit, he wasn't going to last, he thought, as she picked up the pace, looking down into his eyes in wonder. Suddenly, she went wild, throwing her head back, her long hair falling down behind her, caressing his balls; she took him like a wild thing until she screamed her orgasm and collapsed on his chest.

Unable to help himself, he rolled her over, hooked his arms behind her legs and drove into her again and again. She laced her arms around his neck, rising up to meet his every thrust. She came again, looking into his eyes and raking his back with her sharp little claws as he pounded into her. Her orgasm triggered his – he buried himself completely, shuddering over her repeatedly as he pumped his seed into her sweet body. Nickolas knew in that moment that this was the only woman he wasn't going to be able to walk away from. Somehow, some way, he had to tie her to him, because he sure as fuck could never let her go.

He rolled over carefully, leaving her body and drawing her into his arms.

"You Okay?"

"Yes."

"Did I hurt you?"

"No."

They fell silent for a while, just holding on to each other in the aftermath of what had to have been the best sex he'd ever had.

"Agent Pane?"

"Do you suppose you could bring yourself to call me Nickolas?" he asked, a smile in his voice.

"Nickolas?"

"What, baby?"

"I think I may have scratched you."

"Mmm, yes, you did."

"I'm sorry."

"I'm not, it made me hot."

"Oh."

"In fact, talking about it makes me hot and I'm sure you're sore so we had best change the subject. Let's take a quick shower, then we can sleep in my bed; we've made a thorough mess of this one."

"You want to sleep with me?"

"Yes, baby, I want to sleep with you. Will you let me?"

"Yes, I think I would like that."

Thank god; because he didn't know if he could stand to let her out of his sight. For Christ's sake, he had only known her a couple of days. Was this the obsession the other men she had worked with suffered from? Somehow, he knew it was that, but more, much more. As far as he was concerned, she was his at first sight. As he had told her, he wanted her long before she had touched him to contact his brother. Then she had given herself to him, had come apart in his arms. She didn't do that with any of the others. At least he had that to hold onto.

~ CHAPTER FOURTEEN ~

When Talia woke, she found Nickolas showered and dressed in dark suit pants and a dress shirt. He was sitting in the chaise lounge, looking at her with flaming hot, ice-blue eyes. She realized she had never felt so safe or slept so well – hadn't even woken up when he left the bed. She'd never imagined she would be able to sleep with another person present, much less in a man's arms.

"Did I oversleep?" she asked drowsily.

"No, ma'am," he responded, to which she raised an arched blonde eyebrow.

"Agent Pane, I presume?" she asked with a small, cool smile.

"For now," he said, smiling tightly.

"Hmm." She stood from the bed, naked, and stretched, then turned and sashayed toward her room, her luscious ass peeking from behind her long, tousled hair. He was on her in a minute. Grabbing her from behind and lifting her off her feet, he crushed her naked body against his chest and buried his face in her sleep-warmed neck.

"You're playing with fire, woman," he whispered into her hair, then bit down on the cords in her neck.

"Is it Nickolas now?" she asked breathlessly as he carried her back to the bed, laid her down on her back, and then rose over her, pinning her hands above her head.

"I'll be whoever I have to be in order to keep that sweet ass of yours safe," he growled down at her, searching her face. "Do you understand?" She could feel his erection pressing into her bare stomach from behind his wool suit pants.

He'd been in every sort of agony imaginable – waking up with her beautiful naked body wrapped around his. How the fuck was he going to protect her if he couldn't keep his hands off of her? He'd gotten up, taken a cold shower and dressed, before torturing himself further watching her sleep in his bed.

Nickolas knew he'd never been so out of control. If he had a brain in his head, he would turn her over to another agent, but the thought of another man close enough to guard her drove him into a killing rage. Damn, but he was in a world of hurt here, and her life lay in the balance.

"I'll be the first to admit I know next to nothing about men, but unless I miss my guess, that thing you're packing in your pants isn't your gun."

"No, not my gun," he dropped his forehead on hers and groaned.

"To take another wild guess, I'd have to say that 'not-your-gun' is why you find it necessary to be so mean to me this morning."

She was too astute. Was he being mean to her? He didn't want to be mean. Fuck, he was losing it. He couldn't even string two coherent thoughts together when she was under him. He elected not to respond to the obvious.

"You're hurting my wrists, would you mind letting them go?"

82

God, he was being an animal pinning her like that, naked and helpless beneath him. He became aware of the small bones of her wrists crushed together in one of his powerful hands. He'd never manhandled a woman before in his life, yet, every time he turned around, he found himself mauling this one. He let go, sat up on the edge of the bed with his back to her and put his head in his hands. He hated himself – really hated himself in that moment. His feelings were so strong they bled through, and Talia picked up on them.

"We're both out of our element here," she said in a soft voice, getting up on her knees behind him. She surprised him by wrapping her arms around his neck from behind. "Like I said, I really don't know much about men, but I have a suggestion."

He reached up with one large callused hand and gently wrapped his fingers around her forearms where they crossed in front of his neck, holding her to him.

"What's your suggestion?" God knew he was open, being at a loss himself.

"I'd like to have another meet and greet with Nickolas, then you can agent up on me if you must."

"That means I'll take you again, and I don't even know if I can be gentle about it," he confessed.

"I'll endeavor to endure." She reflected his earlier words back at him with a smile in her voice.

"Baby, do you have any idea what you're getting yourself into?" he agonized. "Not only can't I get enough of you, every time I have you I just want you more."

"I don't think trying to resist is going to do either of us any good. If we indulge whenever it's safe to do so, we may – just may – be able to concentrate on the mission between times."

"You say that as if you want me, too."

"I do."

Holy fuck!

"Precisely," she responded to his unspoken explicative as she unbuttoned his dress shirt.

True to his word, Nickolas wasn't gentle about it. He pulled her under him and took her with long forceful thrusts, again and again, until they were both in tears from the repeated orgasms. He never softened – until somewhere around the sixth explosion when he finally collapsed. Gripping her to his chest, he shuddered violently and repeatedly in the most mind blowing orgasm of his life.

She had stayed with him every stroke of the way, wrapping her legs around his hips and clawing his back in her rapture. She'd even bit him several times, and he was sure his shoulder would bear her marks. Marks he was honored to have – evidence of a passion he was proud to have drawn from her. God, but she was one hell of a woman. *His woman.*

"I'm sorry I was rough, did I hurt you, baby?" he asked, bracing himself on his elbows and gently brushing her soft hair from her perfect face. Her lips were swollen from his ravaging kisses, her cheeks pink from his roughened jaw; he'd left a love bite on her ivory throat. She looked up at him like a woman well-loved and shook her head. "Oh, thank god, you strip me of all control." She just smiled and ran her fingers down his face in a tender caress, searched his eyes for a moment, then got out from under him to go shower. He followed suit, heading toward his own shower.

They had to get moving if they were going to catch breakfast before their flight, he thought, digging deep to find Agent Pane somewhere in the sated depths of Nickolas, the enthralled man.

~ CHAPTER FIFTEEN ~

When they boarded the Emirates Airlines A380, Talia was delighted with the privacy of their first class seats. The entire aircraft was decorated in soothing beiges, golds, and tans with rich wood paneling. There was a divider between their seats and the aisle, affording further privacy. Nickolas seated her next to the window, and shielded her by taking the aisle seat. For once, there was plenty of leg room for his long frame.

"We'll be in the air about thirteen hours," he informed her. "Your seat will recline into a bed when you are ready to get some sleep." God knows they didn't get much last night.

She looked over at him. He was wearing a light brown summer suit with a cream dress shirt open at the throat. Quite a change from his dark agent persona, but it looked great on him. She supposed everything would look great on the man, he was so darn handsome. His large left hand was on the arm of his seat next to her. His wedding band stood out against his dark skin. Moved by his thoughtfulness, she impulsively reached over and put her hand on his.

"Thank you, Wade," she said smiling up at him.

Nickolas couldn't have been more surprised. Never before had she reached out to him, much less touched him in public. Sure, it was appropriate to their cover, but still… The impact of that gentle touch made its way through his body and settled in his groin. He braced himself, digging deep for his composure, and waited to see how long she would leave her hand on his.

Classy as always, today she was dressed in a powder blue, drape-necked sleeveless top, and form fitting gray skirt. He caught a glimpse of his mark on her throat exposed by the drape of the blouse, mostly covered by makeup. He couldn't afford to think about what seeing the evidence of their "indulgence" did to him. Black pumps and a large black travel handbag completed Talia's outfit. Her wedding set sparkled in the light where her hand rested on the arm of her seat, filling him with proprietary pride. If he was honest, and he always tried to be brutally honest with himself, he wanted that to be *his* band on her finger, rather than part of a temporary cover. God, he had to get hold of himself.

He put his other hand over hers, leaned down and placed a gentle, lingering kiss on her temple, then lifted her hand and placed it back on her armrest.

"Sorry, I forgot myself," she apologized, looking down in shame.

"Don't be sorry, I love your touch, angel, it's just a little hard on my concentration."

"Do you expect trouble?" she asked so softly it reached his ears only.

"Always, it's my job," he stated.

Is that really all she was to him, a job? she wondered, her heart hurting at the thought. She grew quiet and looked out the window.

They had been in the air for several hours. Talia had waited as long as she could, but really needed the bathroom. At her request, Nickolas touched his lapel.

"Samuels, we are headed your way," he said softly, looking down at Talia as if speaking to her. She smiled up at him as if in response, once again amazing him with her grasp of what was needed at any given moment. He escorted her to the restrooms next to where Samuels was seated, checked to be sure it was secure before allowing her to enter, and took the opportunity to use the one across from hers. He was fast, but when he came out, she was already gone and Samuels' seat was empty.

"What's your location?" he asked his lapel, trying not to let the panic he was feeling enter his voice. Shit! He never panicked, never.

"I followed her back to her seat and am standing at the lounge across from her. All is secure," Samuels answered in his earcom. When Nickolas walked further down the aisle toward their seats, he could see Samuels standing at the bar with a drink in hand. He was facing partly away from Talia so he could see her out of the side of his eye without appearing to be looking her way. He was far enough away, there appeared to be no connection between them, but close enough he would be all over anyone trying to get at her. Talia was looking into a compact mirror, appearing to be applying lip gloss, but he could see she was using it to watch the aisle behind her. Damn, it was nice working with professionals, he thought, as he slipped into the seat beside her.

"You didn't wait for me," he stated.

"The stewardess asked me to take my seat, and I didn't want to make a scene. You know how it is these days with the terroristaphobia," she replied with a little smile.

"You knew Samuels had your back?" He whispered the question in her ear under the ruse of kissing her cheek. He really needed to know more about her training.

"Yes, I know, and I love you, too, Wade," she said, looking up into his eyes meaningfully.

Even though he realized she was answering his question while speaking for the benefit of the steward that just arrived to offer them refreshments, he felt as if she had sucker punched him in the chest. He realized he wanted her love – badly.

Shit!

She resumed looking out of the window in silence for another hour, then reclined her seat and drifted off to sleep. All he could do was watch her in an agony of twisted emotions. How in the hell did this get so fucking jacked up? How did he get so jacked up?

Suddenly her eyes sprang open, and she looked directly at him.

"Agent Carlton thinks we have a problem," she whispered to him just before his ear-com went off.

"There's a drunk headed your way. Something about him doesn't feel right," Carlton informed him over the link.

"It's that man coming down the aisle," she whispered, even though she couldn't have heard what Carlton reported to him over their private com. For that matter, she had never formally met Carlton, nor did she have any way of knowing his name, Nickolas realized.

She slowly returned the seat upright and leaned over him, appearing to be reaching for a magazine. "I passed him on my way back from the bathroom. He may have brushed up against me. If he tries to grab me, let him."

"Like hell!"

"You're going to have to trust me on this one, it's the best way. Besides, I'll be fine, you'll be right here," she said, leaning close and running her fingers down his jaw in apparent affection.

The man was middle aged, very large, apparently very drunk and had Talia in his sights. All the signs of a lust filled obsession blazed out of his bloodshot eyes.

Shit!

He stopped by their seats, had the fucking balls to reach around the partition, right over Nickolas, and grab Talia by the wrist as if the giant agent didn't even exist.

"Come on, baby, I'm going to buy you a drink," he slurred.

Talia made as if to stand up in alarm, placing her free hand on the drunk's chest over his heart as if to balance herself. The man arched, groaned, pissed himself, then, with the help of a subtle shove from Talia, fell to the aisle floor, rather than on Nickolas' lap, where he lay unmoving; unconscious or dead, Nickolas was not sure. Talia threw herself into Nickolas' arms, buried her face in his neck and appeared to cry as alarmed stewards approached from both directions in haste.

"Do you know this man?" The stewardess asked them, looking down at the heap. A guttural snore that rose from the body indicated life still lingered. More's the pity, Nickolas thought uncharitably.

"No, he just staggered over here and accosted my wife, then passed out," Nickolas explained, holding the apparently distraught Talia to his chest. He could see Samuels and Carlton had approached from opposite sides of the cabin and stood some distance behind the stewards in case backup was needed. Seeing things were under control, the agents took their seats in order to not draw attention. Talia sat away from him and reached into her purse, pulling out a small package of tissues. She wiped her eyes, blew her nose, then rested back against him, apparently for further comfort.

A doctor that *happened* to be sitting a few rows down from them offered to look at the man.

"Will he be Okay?" Talia asked, leaning over Nickolas' lap and closer to the doctor in her apparent concern. Only Nickolas could see the small hypodermic she slipped into Wilkinson's palm. She managed to do so without touching the doctor's hand. She must have pulled that out of her purse when she got the tissues, Nickolas realized. How had she gotten that through security? Damn, she was good!

"He just appears to be very drunk," the doctor assured her. "Did he hurt you?"

"No, he just scared me," she sniffled.

The now sedated drunk was hauled to the back of the plane and strapped in next to the steward's station to sleep it off. Apologies were forthcoming from the staff and free drinks delivered to Talia and Nickolas. The incident faded into the background as hors d'oeuvres, free drinks and flight credits were delivered to the rest of the first class passengers that had experienced the disruption.

Nickolas continued to hold Talia against his chest, idly stroking her back. It was what would be expected of a doting husband, he assured himself, but the brutally honest part knew he simply did not want to let her go…ever.

"You Okay?" he finally whispered the question into her hair.

"Right as rain," she whispered back. "Do you think it has been long enough for me to gather my composure, or do we still need the theatrics?" Damn, she was good!

"A little longer, people are still occasionally glancing our way," he responded, more than happy to hold her.

"Are you holding up Okay with me all over you like this?" she asked, concerned.

"It's a tough job, but someone has to do it. I will endeavor to endure." She could hear the smile in his voice and lost another little piece of her heart.

~ CHAPTER SIXTEEN ~

The first class lounge in Dubai was a study in glass walls and open spaces. Talia looked out of one of those windows, the sky so blue as to appear surreal. She was trying not to take in all the things going on in the heads of the people around her.

Nickolas had informed her they had a several hours layover in Dubai, United Arab Emirates before the next leg of their trip, a two hour flight to Ryiadh, Saudi Arabia. From Ryiadh, they had a quick connection that would have them rushing to a one hour domestic flight to Hafr Al Batin where they had a suite of rooms for the night. With the next two flights and the time to get to the hotel, they were still probably five or six hours from finding a bed, which would put it at midnight or one o'clock local time before they could get some shut eye.

So far, Nickolas had not slept. He had been by her side, ever vigilant, for over nineteen hours. Though he didn't show it, he had to be getting tired. They didn't exactly get much sleep the night before.

"Now that we have a little space, why don't you fill me in on what you did to that guy on the plane?" his deep voice interrupted her thoughts. She knew his lack of questioning had been too good to last. Apparently, he had just been biding his time until he could be sure they would not be overheard.

"When I was in the institution, some of the patients were there because they had severe epilepsy. I grew close to one girl about my age. She could not function in society as her grand mal seizures were not controllable. Even deeply medicated, she would suffer them numerous times a week. They were awful to watch and undoubtedly much worse to go through. One day we were alone in the rec room playing a game of cards and she went into a seizure. I jumped from my chair and grabbed her before she could hit the tile floor and split her head open. She was larger than I, so we both ended up going down on the floor. I was able to cushion her fall – and just lay there with her, my arms and legs wrapped around her to keep her from hurting herself until it was over. When I was in such close contact with her I could follow what was happening in her body and in her brain. I learned how to stop the seizure. Apparently, the seizure prevented me from having my normal effect when I touched her. As long as I was with her, I could feel when she was about to have one, and if I was in her field, I could stop it. Needless to say, after that she was glad to hang out with me even though I didn't talk.

"So what does that have to do with the drunk on the plane?" Nickolas wanted to know.

"I'm getting there, you need the background. There was another woman in the institution with us that had what they call vagal nerve syndrome. The vagal nerve helps to regulate the heartbeat, control muscle movement, keep a person breathing, and to transmit a variety of chemicals through the body. It carries incoming information from the nervous system to the brain, providing information about what the body is doing, and it also transmits outgoing information which governs a range of reflex responses. In this woman's case, anything that produced even a mild adrenalin response would affect the vagal nerve causing her heart to stop, and she would pass out. Fortunately, her heart would start back up on its own, but it was so debilitating she had to be institutionalized. One day my friend asked me if I could help the other woman as I had her. The next time her friend had an episode, I got close enough to be in her field and traced what was going on. I was able to stop her incidents as well, as long as I was with her when they came on. In both cases, I used electrical impulses from my nervous system, passed them through my field into the women's bodies, and corrected what was shorting out in their nervous systems. With me so far?"

"I think so."

"There was a male aide on my ward that I didn't trust. He had the misfortune of having bumped into me in the hall once, and his hand made contact with my bare arm. He was becoming increasingly amorous, if you know what I mean."

"Yes, I would have to say I have firsthand knowledge of the phenomena."

"One evening, he grabbed me and pulled me into a bathroom and tried to rape me."

"Bastard!" Nickolas growled.

"I was really scared and just reacted. I put my hand on his chest to shove him off of me and it just happened."

"What happened?"

"I found out my little trick could work in reverse as well. This time the electrical current went directly from my hand and stopped his heart."

"Did it start back up again?" Nickolas was almost afraid to ask.

"No."

"Oh."

"Indeed."

She looked back out the window. They sat in silence for quite some time.

"You didn't have to tell me that, you know," Nickolas said, watching her closely. It was obvious it hadn't been easy for her.

"Yes, I felt I did," she responded without looking away from the window.

"Why?"

"There may very well be a time when both of our lives depend upon you knowing exactly what I am capable of."

"Does anyone else know?'"

"Very few; it's classified."

"You apparently have had an opportunity to refine the technique."

"Yes, Dr. Wilkinson helped me under very controlled conditions. That's how we figured out exactly what it was I did." Still, she had not looked at him. He could feel her pulling away.

"Look at me," he instructed. Slowly, she turned her head from the window and met his eyes in challenge. Hers were full of resigned despair. He could tell she was bracing herself for his rejection. He reached out and wrapped his fingers around her nape, and placed his thumb on the bottom of her jaw. His hand was huge next to her small face. "With a small amount of pressure and the appropriate twist of my wrist, you are dead. Do you understand me?" She slowly nodded, searching his eyes. "I can kill you with a touch in over a hundred ways. Understand?" Again the nod. "Are you afraid of me?"

"No, but you are not a monster," she responded.

"And neither are you."

The small tear that appeared in her eye broke his heart. He pulled her to him and held her to his chest. Reflexively, her small hand came up over his heart. He put his other hand over it and held it against him. Nothing could have made Talia feel more trusted or accepted. Just touching her had to be torture for him, and her hand over his heart in light of their discussion had to be threatening, yet he held her as if she were just a normal woman in need of comfort. Her heart was clearly more at risk than his where it beat strong and steady under her palm.

~ CHAPTER SEVENTEEN ~

Talia had managed to catch an hour nap on the Emirates flight from Ryiadh to Dubai as they had reclining first class seats, but the domestic flight to Hafr Al-batin had been on a modern but small Embraer EMB 170 jet. It was maxed out at seventy passengers with people seated two on each side of a narrow isle.

As they took their seats, a can of sardines came to mind. Nickolas was reduced to leaving his long legs in the aisle and taking up part of her seat with his broad shoulders. Thankfully the flight had only been an hour long, the Hafr Al-batin airport small and easy to negotiate and a taxi readily available. They were so crammed together during the flight that not touching her had been impossible, and his desire for her was riding him hard. That and twenty five hours with no sleep, had his control shaky at best.

Their suite was at a Holiday Inn. There apparently had not been much to choose from in the smaller town. Fortunately, it was upscale, clean, airy and light with off-white walls and carpet, white bed spread and tan curtains and accents. Large oak double doors closed off the bedroom from the living room where there was a sleeper couch for his use. He hoped those doors had a sturdy lock because she was going to need it if she planned to keep him off of her, he mused. Nickolas tipped the bellboy, then closed and locked the suite's outer door. He did not turn around right away, but stood, his large frame facing the door, trying to gather himself.

"Nickolas?" she ventured in a concerned voice.

"Yes, I'm afraid Agent Pane signed off duty," he responded.

"Oh," she answered getting his drift. "Good, he was showing signs of getting grumpy." She walked up behind him, wrapped her arms around his waist and put her cheek against the middle of his broad back.

"You must be exhausted," he ventured between gritted teeth. "You take the bedroom and I'll bunk out here on the couch."

"I thought we had an agreement," she stated.

"What agreement?" God, if she didn't get away from him soon he was going to forget all his good intentions and take her in the entryway.

"To indulge ourselves whenever it was safe. We are safe in here, are we not?"

Shit, he hadn't even checked out the rooms, he realized. He turned to do so, but she didn't move. His action brought her flush up against his tight chest and full erection.

"I have to secure our quarters," he informed her, taking her by the shoulders and setting her back from him.

"We're alone," she assured him.

Alone....Oh, god... Swallowing hard, he forced himself away from her, pulled his Beretta from his shoulder holster, and secured every room before returning. She was still standing in the living room where he had left her.

"Do you feel better now?" she asked with a small smile, kicking off her pumps.

Better? Not hardly. How could a woman removing her shoes be so damn sexy? She walked up to him and started unbuttoning his shirt. When he clamped his big hand over hers to still her action, she looked up into his eyes questioningly.

"Are you going to be able to sleep with that 'not-your-gun' in your pants?" she asked, glancing down at his tented suit slacks.

"Probably not. No." Even though he was in a serious hurt, he had to smile at her comment. His smile rapidly faded, however, when she resumed unbuttoning his shirt. "Talia, baby," he implored, wrapping his hand around her busy little fingers, "I have zero control, I don't want to run the risk of hurting you."

"I'm not as fragile as I look. I promise I won't break, Nickolas," she whispered, looking deeply into his eyes.

"Ah shit, baby," he groaned, sweeping her up and carrying her to the bedroom. He could no more stop himself now than he could stop breathing. He had to have her. She wrapped her arms around his thick neck and nuzzled against it as his long, determined strides carried her to the bed. He had to make it to the bed, damn it, he was *not* going to take her on the floor – or against the wall, or…..

He placed her in the center of the bed and started unwrapping her like a precious package, his big hands shaking with the control he was exerting in an attempt not to rip her clothes from her sweet body. She reached up and pushed his suit jacket off his broad shoulders. He paused just long enough to shed it and kick off his shoes. When he turned around, she'd managed to lose her skirt and lay there in nothing but matching scraps of baby blue lace. Oh, god! She sat up, reached for his belt, unbuckled it, unzipped his pants and took him in her little soft hand.

"You're so large, it's amazing we fit together," she marveled as she ran her fingers across the steel incased in velvet.

"Baby!" he groaned. "You just can't do that, I'm not going to last." He stepped away from her magic hand and all but ripped the rest of his clothes off. "I've never wanted anything like I want you," he confessed, looking down at this beautiful woman. HIS beautiful woman, everything in him insisted. He reached down and gently removed the pins from her hair, freeing her waist length platinum mane. "I want to feel this on my skin," he said in a husky, strained voice as he ran a lock of her hair between his fingers. His knees almost gave way at the memory of it flowing down her back and pooling on his balls while she went wild on top of him.

He joined her on the bed, slipped the bra straps off her shoulders, and pulled the cups off her gorgeous full breasts so they were plumped up from underneath. Leaning over, he took one pert, pink nipple into his mouth. She threw back her head, arched into his mouth, sank her fingers into his hair and pulled him closer. God, but he wanted to eat her alive. He forced himself to gentle when he wanted to devour her, mark her as his. He managed to remove the bra and pull the lace thong over her hips and off her long legs without ripping them. He lay on his back, and with a show of casual strength, lifted her entire body by her waist and placed her over his prone form. He positioned himself at her wet entrance, but let her make the next move. He really couldn't trust himself not to ravage her at this point, and he would rather die than hurt her again.

She placed both small hands on his chest to brace herself, then slowly sank down on him while looking into his eyes. He lost it and grabbed her hips, thrusting up until he was totally buried in her trembling body.

"Oh, god, baby, I'm sorry," he groaned, trying to let go of her and slow down. It was not to be. All control gone, he lifted her up and slammed her down on his raging cock, drawing a gasp from her. He could feel her muscles spasm around his invasion. Straddling his large frame, her body was open and vulnerable to his mercy, and he had none – only raging desire to take her so hard and so deep she would never be free of him.

He flipped her over on her back in one powerful motion and mantled over her, driving in again. She wrapped her long legs around his hips and buried her face in his throat, whimpering– whether in fear, pain or desire, he couldn't tell. He took her endlessly with long, hard, deep strokes, leaving no corner of her depths unplumbed.

"You. Are. Mine." he forcefully stated, bracing himself on his thick muscular arms in order to look into her face. "Say it, Talia, say you are mine," he demanded, punctuating every word with another deep, circular thrust. Her eyes flashed hot into his, her neck arched as passion overtook her and she came for him. Shudder after contracting shudder rippled through her core, gripping him inside her, and still he took her with deep, pounding thrusts. She came again, her heels hitting the bed and her entire body arching up into him.

"Say it, damn you, Talia, say you're mine." His thrusts were brutal now, granting her no quarter. He was so deep she felt her womb cramping in protest. He reared back on his heels, drawing her to him with both hands on her pelvis, arching her back and granting him the ultimate penetration. The pain/pleasure of his savage assault threw her into another blinding orgasm, and all she could do was scream incoherently, thrashing her head from side to side, sinking her nails into his powerful forearms. Wave after orgasmic wave crashed over her as she fought for her next breath and looked into his powerful face. His features were drawn tight, teeth grinding, mouth almost cruel, but his laser blue eyes were desperate, pleading, full of roiling emotions she couldn't identify as his body continued to piston into her.

"Say it," he all but sobbed.

"I am yours, Nickolas, there will be no other," she managed to get out between gasps.

As if her words had freed him, he drove up into her one last time. Every muscle locked tight as time seemed to stand still. He poured his scalding seed deep into her body in an endless driving orgasm. He wrapped one powerful arm around the small of her back, drawing her up to straddle his lap. Crushing her into his muscular chest, his cock was still buried deep, pulsing his seed. She came again, sinking her teeth into the thick cords of his neck.

~

He ran them a bath in the oversized jet tub, carried her limp, sated body to the bathroom and sank down into the warm water with her in his arms. He hadn't spoken, just held her as if he couldn't bring himself to let her go. Finally he took up a small bar of fragrant French milled soap and gently bathed her.

"Have I damaged you?" he asked, as he ever so carefully ran his soapy fingers through her swollen folds.

"No, but I think you stopped my heart a couple of times," she smiled at him in reassurance.

"I was a fucking animal. There is no excuse for it." His voice was full of self loathing and regret.

"I love the way you are with me, Nickolas, you take my breath away."

He searched her face for some time, as if to test the sincerity of her words before pulling her head into his chest.

"I know I forced the words from you under duress, but I'm still going to hold you to them. You are mine, Talia. I won't let you go. Do you understand me?"

"I *will* see you through this, Nickolas, I promise."

"That's just it. I don't want 'through this.' I want you," he countered in an agonized whisper, holding her so tightly she could hardly breathe. "God, I sound like one of your fucking stalkers. You must hate me."

"No."

"No what?"

"No, I don't hate you."

He dried them both and carried her back to bed.

"I can walk, you know. Besides, I need to get a gown," she informed him through a yawn.

"No."

"No what?" It was her turn to ask.

"Negative on the gown. I want to sleep against your naked body with your hair all over me."

"Okay."

Oh, thank god! He was in such a tangle he didn't even know himself. All he could hope was that some sleep would set him right, but the thought of sleeping without her in his arms caused him physical pain. He was beginning to feel distinctly like an addict.

Several times during the night, she woke with him making tender, gentle love to her. She readily received him into her body as they came together in rolling waves of ecstasy, before falling back into an exhausted sleep with him still inside her.

Being with her was unlike anything he had ever experienced – so far beyond sex, he couldn't describe what they shared. He'd been so wild, so forceful with her the first time that night, he knew she must be sore, but she never turned from him or turned him away. Impossibly, her passion seemed to match his, her powerful orgasms milking his from the depths of his soul.

~

Fortunately, their itinerary gave them plenty of time to sleep in. It was noon, local time when they finally ordered brunch delivered to their room. Dr. Wilkinson was scheduled to meet them in their suite at two o'clock that afternoon to monitor Talia while she connected with Nickolas' brother again. Once she got a bearing on his current location, plans would be made for their departure that evening to find him. The next leg of their journey would most likely be trans-desert, not something one wanted to start at high noon in a Saudi Arabian summer.

She sat across the dining table from him with one leg drawn up under her, dressed in matching soft white cotton drawstring pants and loose fitting scooped neck top. Her hair was down, pulled back with a white scarf headband. She looked painfully young and innocent as she greedily devoured her omelet.

"Sorry we missed dinner," he apologized.

"Quite all right, you were worth the sacrifice," she responded, amazing him.

He could hardly believe she actually enjoyed his wild possession of her when less than three days ago she'd been an untried virgin. The woman was totally beyond his experience. He loved her open, honest response to him and her teasing manner. He loved her competency in the field and her cool head under fire. In fact, so far there was nothing about her he had found that he didn't love. The thought was a sobering one.

He almost dreaded their upcoming session with his brother. God knew he was anxious to find him, but the memory of his condition on their last encounter and what it did to Talia had him fearing for both of them. The time it had taken to get this close to Daniel's locale had chafed, but Nickolas understood that time was being used to get an extraction team in place and an escape route set.

~ CHAPTER EIGHTEEN ~

She was back, he was sure of it. Slowly Daniel opened his swollen, bloodshot green eyes and there she was, shimmering in front of him, ethereal and beautiful, dressed in white.

"Talia?" he croaked.

"You know my name?" she asked, surprised.

"Yes, I heard Nickolas say it. Are you the enemy?"

"No, Daniel, I'm not your enemy. I'm with Nickolas, and we're going to find you."

"How?" Daniel wanted to know.

"I'll need your help."

"I don't know where I am," he reminded her.

"That's Okay, all you have to do is try to stay awake, and let me see through you," she assured him.

"There's not much to see," he said, then remembered the decaying hand. "No! You don't want to see in here, don't look."

"It's Okay, Daniel, I already see it."

"Oh, god," he moaned.

"Just try to stay present for me, Okay?"

"WILCO," he whispered, struggling to maintain consciousness.

Talia hooked into Daniel before doing what she had come to call her "Google Earth" thing. Using him to anchor her location, she drifted up and out of the building to get a higher perspective with her remote viewing.

"I see a set of four small cinderblock buildings. They look like supply buildings, have no windows and are probably only 15' X 15'. They appear old, as if they've been there a long time. They have flat, tar roofs that are worse for wear with sand drifted into the corners. A little ways off are some tents. There are Arab men carrying assault rifles – so far, I count eight of them. I don't see any vehicles. Wait – there they are – three trucks of some sort, covered with desert camo net tarp," she relayed to the men in the room.

"Turning now to check the sun for orientation and going up higher. Mostly flat desert with no particular land marks. From up here the buildings seem to be in a slight draw of some sort. Leading part way up to the buildings on the southwest is a narrow dirt road. It must be really old as parts of it are drifted over. Going higher... Bingo! I see a highway to the northwest. It doesn't connect to the dirt road. Near as I can tell, the dirt road doesn't connect to anything anymore. I have enough for now and Daniel is fading. I need to see to him."

"Talia, just come back, we can't risk you," Dr. Wilkinson instructed her.

"No, not yet, I don't think he'll last without a little support. I'll be careful. I know how much I can afford," she said, taking a firmer grip on Nickolas' hand.

A short time later she awoke to find herself in Nickolas' arms, looking up into his concerned face.

"Hey," she said.

"Hey yourself. So much for knowing what you can afford to do." She could tell he was angry.

"How long have I been out?"

"Too damn long," Nickolas snarled.

"About ten minutes," Wilkinson informed her, removing the blood pressure cuff from her arm with practiced, gloved hands.

"Do you remember any of what you saw?" Agent Samuels wanted to know. He was sitting in front of a laptop next to a bunch of hi tech equipment that afforded a direct satellite connection.

"She has a photographic memory," Wilkinson informed the agent.

"Handy," Samuels responded, impressed by the petite blonde.

"I relayed the information from her trance to recon, but so far it isn't enough to go on," Agent Carlton informed them. He was wearing a headset, sitting across the table in front of an impressive bank of portable communications equipment.

"I've pulled up a satellite map of the area. Whenever you're feeling recovered enough, you can take a look," Samuels said, regarding her in concern.

"I'm good," she responded.

"Bullshit!" Nickolas countered.

"Well, I'm good enough; we have to get this show on the road. I was only able to do so much for Daniel and every moment counts," she snarled back, more than sick of his surly attitude. She stood up to her full height, all of five foot two, then ruined the effect by swaying on her feet. Nickolas lifted and carried her to the chair next to Samuels, then took a post behind her like a towering sentinel.

"Must you hulk?" she asked irritably, looking back at him with flashing gray eyes.

"Yes, I must," he snapped back, glaring at her with his icy laser blues.

"Now, children, can we proceed?" Samuels asked, tongue in cheek.

"Sure thing, daddy," Nickolas responded without rancor. Talia let out an exaggerated sigh and turned her attention to the computer screen.

"We're here," Samuels gestured, indicating Hafar Al Batin on the map with a long dark finger.

"I was able to view back to here," she informed him, pointing to a highway. "It looks like, to get there from here, we need to take highway 85 west to Al Jumaymah. From there, follow this smaller road heading almost due north across the Saudi/ Iraqi border." She indicated an unmarked road on the map. "Follow it to here, just east of Ash Shabakah. See this little jog in the road? Just before the jog, see this faint line right here going off to the southeast? It looks like a draw or something. There's a dirt road running along here that fades in and out. The buildings sit just off to the northeast, here," she finished, tapping the screen with a polished nail.

"I don't know what you're doing after this gig, but I sure could use you on my team. You'd make a great addition to my other equipment," he said, indicating his computer setup. "Maybe I'll just pull some strings and get you transferred," Samuels complimented, drawing a feral snarl from Nickolas.

"Tough luck, buckaroo, she's not enlisted," Nickolas growled.

"Oh, I'm sure with her skills, that could be arranged with no problem," Samuels countered, his fingers flying over the keyboard. "Latitude 30.8974, longitude 43.8749," he called out to Carlton. "In fact, I could probably arrange it from here," he teased, indicating the computer.

"Do, and die," Nickolas stated in a low growl.

"Roger that," Carlton acknowledged the coordinates.

"You want me dead, too? What has your balls in an uproar over there?" Samuels asked.

"Not that, numb nuts, the coordinates," Carlton called back. "Stick with me here, partner." Then into his headset, "Copy base, latitude 30.8974, longitude. 43.8749, over."

"Pulling it up real-time," Samuels stated as the map on the computer screen flickered before zooming in. "Is this the place?" he asked Talia.

"Yes, that's it," she confirmed.

"Okay, get ready to rock, boys and girl, they will pick us up en route," Samuels instructed. "Hey, Nickolas, my man, how do you look in a thawb?"

"Oh, he's going to be absolutely darling!" Talia teased on her way to the bedroom to change.

115

"A what?" Nickolas wanted to know.

"It's kinda like a white night shirt, darling, I can hardly wait to see you in it," Talia called from behind the bedroom door.

"No fucking way!" Nickolas protested.

"Don't forget your sunglasses. Those baby blue peepers will blow your cover," Carlton advised, packing up his gear.

"Yeah, and wrap the ghutrah around that white mug of yours while you're at it," Samuels added on his way out the door, computer gear already packed into his black duffel.

"See you back at base. Take good care of her, Pane," Dr. Wilkinson said, before leaving as well.

~

When Talia came back into the living room, Nickolas did a double take. Gone was the blonde bombshell and in her place was a Muslim woman. Dark brown eyes with black liner looked back at him from under dark brows, the only features of her face still visible behind her veil. The rest of her was draped in black from head to sandaled feet. Her hands and feet, the only other parts of her body visible, appeared to be dark skinned. Her nails were now short and free of polish. She carried a cloth satchel.

"Your wardrobe awaits you," she said from behind her veil, indicating the bedroom with a sweeping hand.

Nickolas looked on the bed and, sure enough, there was a long, white, collarless nightshirt. Next to it was a large, square, woven red and white checkered scarf and black cotton circles with tassels. Leather sandals with black tire-tread bottoms rested on the floor.

Shit!

"Indeed."

After he was dressed, she helped him put on the damn scarf and black band, called a ghutrah. He had to sit down so she could reach his head. After wrapping the scarf around the lower half of his face, she slipped his sunglasses over his eyes.

"Voilà, Abdulla," she teased him, handing him his papers.

"I'm glad you're enjoying yourself," he grumbled. "It seems everyone is having fun at my expense today."

"Remember to take shorter steps," she advised, turning toward the door.

"What?" he asked as he stood up to follow her out, almost falling on his face when the narrow shirt bound him up at the ankles.

"Shit!"

"Well, if you must, but be sure to use your left hand to wipe," she threw over her shoulder.

When they stepped into the hall, she stopped, then took up a place several paces behind him.

"I need you in front where I can see you," he reminded her.

"Sorry, you'll have to grow eyes in the back of your head. A good Muslim wife walks two paces behind her husband. We wouldn't want me to get stoned, would we?"

The mental image of her flat on her back in harem garb smoking a hookah brought a smile to his lips, so he shared the image with her.

"I mean with rocks, you dolt," she laughed.

That image he did not find so funny.

~ CHAPTER NINETEEN ~

Samuels and Carlton were waiting in front of the hotel in a beat up Toyota. In their thawbs, ghutrahs and swarthy skin, they looked more like natives than the natives. Fortunately, the AC was in good working order, Talia noticed, as she and Nickolas got into the back seat. The drive promised to be long and hot.

The light was beginning to fade from a cloudless sky when Samuels pulled over to the side of the deserted road. There was nothing to be seen but sand and more sand, the same as it had been the entire trip. Not so much as a blade of grass broke the monotony.

"They will pick us up here just before dark," Carlton informed them, consulting his GPS.

About fifteen minutes later, the light was almost gone when they heard helicopters. Four fully armed Kiowa Warriors appeared, flying low and fast. One landed to the side of the road and Talia and the three men rushed to climb in. As soon as the foursome was seated, the chopper was in the air banking to the northeast. Talia was seated between Samuels and Nickolas on a bench seat that ran the entire length of the back of the chopper, with Carlton across from them. They shared the space with Navy Seals in desert camo and full combat gear.

Talia pulled off her veil and stripped out of her black robes. She was wearing desert camo cargo pants and shirt underneath. Reaching into her duffel, she pulled out sox and boots, and put them on. Her long hair was in a French braid down her back, which she wrapped up and tucked under a camo helmet she had also pulled out of her satchel. Leaning over, she pulled the brown contact lenses out of her eyes and applied eye drops from her bag.

Talia was handed a military issue camo holster with a .45 Sig Sauer Auto and extra clips which she dutifully strapped on.

Nickolas, Samuels and Carlton had been provided with desert camo uniforms and helmets, into which they changed with efficient movements. All three men were armed to the teeth. Nickolas had just checked his own Beretta when he looked up to see Talia being armed.

"You know how to use that?" he asked. She gave him a droll stare in response, proceeding to check the clip and put a bullet in the chamber before returning the handgun to the holster with efficient, practiced moves.

When the same soldier handed her what looked to be plastic explosives, Nickolas really started to worry.

"She's to stay on board, right?" he asked the apparent head of the special ops team.

"No, sir. She'll be with us in the second wave for search and rescue," he responded.

"You've got to be kidding!" Nickolas all but shouted. "She can't weigh one-ten soaking wet!"

"Ninety-eight, to be exact," Talia calmly corrected.

"What in the hell do you think you're doing?" he asked, taking her by the shoulders.

"Saving lives, Nickolas. It's what I do, remember?"

"No, I don't remember. I thought you were civilian. You were just to locate the men."

"No."

"No what?"

"No, I am not civilian and I locate and retrieve, as in search and rescue."

"Talia, baby, no, it's too dangerous."

"Do you remember what the General said about the advantages of working with a professional?" she asked him.

"Yes, I vaguely remember something about that," Nickolas responded, confused.

"Well, don't let me down. I trust you to have my six."

There was no more time for debate. They were on site and being bombarded with mortar rounds from the ground. Two of the heavily armed Kiowa Warriors led the formation, taking out ground-to-air on the first pass. Their chopper touched down, and they hit the ground running while another bird covered them from the air, picking off armed Taliban as they tried to rush them from all sides.

"That building – second on the left," Talia called out to the two Seals who were running interference in front of her. They changed direction to where she indicated, all running full out in a serpentine pattern. Damn, the woman was good, Nickolas had to admit, as he actually struggled to keep up with their rapid changes in direction.

Just as they reached the building, a Taliban armed with an assault rifle stepped out from the side and opened fire. One of the two soldiers in front went down. Nickolas dove into Talia's back, driving her to the ground under him while mowing the assailant down with his M16. She scrambled out from under him and continued forward to the downed man in a military crawl.

"Where are you hit?" she demanded.

"My leg, ma'am," the man groaned, holding the inside of his thigh where blood pumped through his fingers.

Shit, it had to be an artery to be spurting like that, Nickolas realized. The poor kid was done for.

He looked at Talia in time to see her eyes glow in the dark. When he looked back at the downed man, the bleeding had stopped.

"Take him to the medics and send backup, we have it from here," she instructed the other Seal. "Nickolas, cover him," she ordered as the man threw his partner over his shoulder and headed back at a dead run.

Reaching into one of her pockets, she pulled out a small packet and attached it to the padlock on the door. Nickolas dropped a Taliban firing on the retreating Seal and then another heading their way.

"Stand back," she instructed, and a small explosion blew the lock off the door.

She pulled her handgun and crouched around the door jam in fighting stance at full draw. Nickolas saw the Sig jump in her hand and fire flash out of the muzzle. It was followed by a grunt and the sound of a body hitting the dirt. Talia disappeared into the dark room.

How the hell had she known one of the enemy was in there? The door had been padlocked from the outside.

"Daniel?" he heard her call out to his brother.

"Over here," was the raspy response.

"Nickolas, he's tied up and I don't want to touch him. Give me your rifle. I'll stabilize him, then cover you while you get him out of here."

As Nickolas handed her his M16, he saw her eyes glow again. He could hear his brother's breathing ease. Bending down, he pulled his knife and cut Daniel's bonds. God, Daniel was a mess. They obviously had worked him over again, but good. He saw the withered, rotting hand on the floor just before Daniel grabbed for it. Relief washed over Nickolas when his brother grabbed the rotting appendage with both of his own.

"Leave it, bro, I have to get you out of here," he instructed.

"No, it's Sam's, got to take him home. Promised myself…"

"Okay, Okay, I've got you," Nickolas assured him as he threw him over his shoulder in a fireman's carry. Talia stepped out the door in front of him and the M-16 went off as she scattered a line of fire into an approaching group of Taliban.

"Go, go, go, go!" she yelled at him. "I've got you covered."

Nickolas ran with his brother on his back. Another Taliban rushed him from the left, but Talia, true to her word, dropped the man before he could fire at them. Medics rushed to him as he approached the chopper and relieved him of Daniel. They put his brother on a stretcher and loaded him into the fifth chopper. Nickolas turned for Talia, but she was no longer behind him.

Then he heard another small explosion. Damn the woman, she had seen them to safety and then gone back.

"Give me another weapon," he demanded, and one was thrown to him from the chopper. He ran to the place he'd heard the explosion, another small building, while locking and loading the M-16. As he approached, he heard her barking orders. Thank god, she was alive.

"Go, go, go!" he heard her yell, and another GI with a man on his back rushed from the building. Talia followed behind with the rifle up to her shoulder, covering him.

"Talia!" he called to her.

"Nickolas, thank god! There's another one in here. Come help me!" she shouted, then turned and went back inside.

"Yes, Ma'am," he muttered. Damn, but she was next to impossible to protect.

Her eyes were already glowing when he entered and found the one handed man lying on the floor. God, he was in bad shape, even worse than Daniel. He'd been beaten until he was barely recognizable. One hand had been severed, the stump dipped in hot tar to stop the bleeding so he could be beaten some more, no doubt. He looked back at Talia in time to see her sway on her feet. She recovered herself before he could reach her.

"Get him out of here, Nickolas. Tell them he needs O pos. stat. I've got you covered."

"Come with me this time, Talia," he ordered.

"I'm right behind you," she assured him.

She never promised to stay behind him, he realized as the scenario repeated. He ran toward the fourth building. Gunfire had tapered off as most of the enemy had been dispatched. He could see three other men being carried on stretchers surrounded by armed Seals covering the evac, but no Talia. He burst into the building, frantic to find her. She was standing stock still in the back. In front of her, a man hung from the rafters by his dislocated arms swaying gently. Blood dripped and pooled on the dirt floor beneath him. As Nickolas drew closer, he could see the poor bastard had been virtually skinned alive.

"Please, put a bullet in my head, I beg you," the bloody mass pleaded in a raspy whisper.

Shit, he was still alive.

Talia was frozen, he realized. She couldn't save the man, nor could she bring herself to kill him.

"Talia?" Nickolas called to her.

She didn't respond.

"Talia, baby, come here. Let the others cut him down, you can't help him."

Her eyes started to glow, and Nickolas took her to the floor.

"I'm sorry, baby, I can't let you do it," he apologized, using a pressure point, rendering her unconscious.

~ CHAPTER TWENTY ~

She had not spoken. It had been weeks, but she just sat in the hospital chair and looked out the window, limp hands, and palms up in her lap, saying nothing. She would not make eye contact. They had told him it was a rare form of catatonia. The prognosis was not good.

To a man, the POWs had been in bad shape and wouldn't have survived transport. Without her stabilizing them, they would have lost virtually all. As it was, the only casualties had been Carlton, the last man she'd located, and, for all intents and purposes, Talia.

She had no one. No one but he dared even touch her, and he could not reach her at all.

"No change?" Daniel asked from the door of her room where he leaned on his walker, IV dangling from its cart beside him.

Thanks to Talia, Daniel was alive, though he was not expected to fully recover. One knee had been badly damaged, and he would probably never jump again.

"No, no change," Nickolas answered, running his fingers through his thick brown hair.

"You love her." It was a statement.

"Yeah." There was no point trying to deny it. He loved her, for all the good it did either of them now.

"They're going to let me out of here next week. I'll be on medical leave for a while. Let's pull some strings and take her home," his brother advised. "She isn't getting any better in here. Maybe the ranch can do what the doctors can't."

Damn, but his kid brother was wise for his years.

~

It was quasi-legal, and he was sure his little national treasure would not approve, but after getting heads together with Daniel, Dr. Wilkinson and the General, they'd managed to get Nickolas and Talia declared as common-law. They had represented themselves as husband and wife, and traveled internationally as such. It was the only way Nickolas could get custody of her. He'd kidnap her before he'd let her become a ward of the state again.

As her common-law husband, he was able to have all of her belongings moved to the ranch, including two very traumatized tomcats. It saddened him how little she had beyond the grouchy felines. There had been no photographs of family. She had none. No memorabilia or knickknacks. Everything had been simply utilitarian. Now he understood why she had said they didn't trust her to dress according to cover. Her wardrobe consisted of jeans and t-shirts, interspersed with a few sweaters. Her life had indeed been hollow and empty. The government had used her, then thrown her away.

Nickolas had gone through the clothes he brought from her home. Armed with the sizes he found in her garments, he lovingly went shopping for her. He bought her soft gowns, robes, and slippers, lacy bras and underwear, soft sweaters and designer jeans. He even included some of the classy skirts, tops and pumps she wore undercover. Lotions, potions, perfumes, soaps, shampoo and conditioner, the whole works. He threw away her bar of Dove, jar of Ponds, and Wal-Mart shampoo. He had more than enough to keep her in luxury the rest of her life, and he intended to do just that.

He moved her things into the master, "his" bedroom. There was a small room off the master, used as a nursery for he and his brother as infants. He set up a bed for himself in that room. He really wanted to sleep with her in his arms, but it felt too much like taking advantage of her. He would wait until she was able to give him permission. That she might never be able to, he refused to consider.

Nickolas was on the family ranch when the day Daniel and Talia would be released finally arrived. They'd been transferred to Fitzsimmons Army Medical Center in Denver, somewhat closer to home. Not that the ranch out in the middle of bum-fuck Wyoming was close to anything. Hell, it was four hours on dirt roads from anywhere significant. He had packed a duffel in case he had to be gone overnight, and set it by the front door of the ranch house.

"Is this ready to be loaded?" Hawk asked from the door. The man was six foot six, big boned and dark skinned. His straight black hair hung to the middle of his back and was tied back with a leather thong at his nape. Startling blue eyes, the exact replica of Nickolas', shown from his dark, chiseled face. He looked to be in his early thirties.

Hawk was Nickolas' cousin on his mother's side, and ranch foreman. He was Nickolas' uncle's son, half Lakota on his birth mother's side. They had virtually been brought up together after Hawk's mother had died giving still birth to his sister when Hawk had been seven. His father had brought the grieving Hawk to his sister to raise, then drank himself into an early grave. Hawk's Lakota grandfather had hired on as a ranch hand in order to help with the boy's upbringing. The old man still worked the ranch tirelessly. Nickolas was grateful to have Hawk as foreman. He trusted him implicitly and respected him greatly.

"Yeah, I probably won't need it, but you can be sure we'll get stuck in town if I don't take it. Are you prepared for an R.O.N.?"

"That agent code for 'staying overnight'?" Hawk teased his cousin. "Yeah, I can manage."

Hawk loaded the duffle beside his own in the back of the Land Rover and slid behind the wheel. Nickolas joined him, and they headed off to the dirt strip and Quonset hanger a mile and a half from the ranch house. Both men got out and pulled the turbo Cessna from the hanger. Hawk performed the preflight check, while Nickolas drove the Rover to herd the sheep off the dirt strip.

The sun was just coming up when Hawk skillfully banked the plane and cleared the red cliff that paralleled the landing strip, setting course for Casper. While the private plane was faster than most, commercial jets were much faster. They planned to take a commercial from Casper to Denver, pick up Daniel and Talia at Fitzsimmons, take a return flight to Casper, then fly the Cessna back to the ranch. It would make for a long day, but Nickolas decided the peace and quiet of the ranch would be better for Talia than spending more time than absolutely necessary in the crowded city.

While Nickolas was an excellent pilot himself, Hawk was better. The man seemed to be one with the air. Nickolas was glad to have him flying when they had Talia onboard so he could focus entirely on her care. She had improved enough that she could bathe and feed herself, but she had to be reminded to eat numerous times during any meal. She could also walk now and willingly followed wherever he led when he took her by the hand or arm, but she never spoke nor met anyone's eyes. It would be her first time in the air since her transfer to Fitzsimmons, and though Nickolas was with her, she shook uncontrollably the entire trip. He hoped that flying commercial, then private, would be easier on her than the military transport

130

had been, but he wanted to be able to focus on her in case she suffered another bout of PTSD.

"Thanks for being there for me, coz," Nickolas addressed Hawk in a rare show of appreciation. They had always been close, working together like well-oiled machinery, neither of them giving it any thought.

"No problem," Hawk said, glancing over at him in surprise. "I look forward to meeting your woman."

"You know she's still mostly unresponsive."

"Yes, well, the land has its own magic. It's good you are bringing her home," Hawk responded in his enigmatic, native way.

"There's something else about her you need to know," Nickolas said, pausing to find the right words. "It's really important that you never touch her without gloves on. Never touch her, skin to skin."

Hawk looked at him from under his reflective aviator glasses with one dark brow raised, waiting for him to expound.

"She has these gifts – well, more like a curse really... I'm not making much sense here, am I?" Nickolas struggled.

"Go on," Hawk encouraged.

"To touch her is to want her forever." There, he'd gotten it out, Nickolas thought, waiting to see what Hawk would make of that.

"Want her how?" Hawk asked.

"Like a man wants a beautiful woman," Nickolas stated baldly.

"I have heard of such," Hawk shocked Nickolas by saying. "She-that-must-not-be-touched."

"No one knows what she is or how she can do the things she does. You've heard of someone like her?" Nickolas grilled his cousin.

"Among my mother's people there are many legends. It would be best we speak with my grandfather; he knows them much better than I," Hawk said, and turned his focus to flying the plane. Nickolas knew the man well enough to know that was all he would get out of him on the subject, so he let it drop.

~

They landed at a fixed-base operator in Casper, Wyoming where they had the Cessna fueled and put into a hangar, then taken a shuttle to the main terminal where a commercial flight took them to Denver International Airport. From there a military limo picked them up and took them to Fitzsimmons. So far everything had gone without a hitch.

Daniel was sitting in a chair in Talia's room, his duffel packed and next to him when Nickolas and Hawk walked in.

"Damn, bro, I forgot what you two monsters looked like in jeans and cowboy boots. What are you trying to do, scare the nurses?" Daniel teased the two giant men. The heels on their dress boots did add to their height, Nickolas realized, having never given it much thought before.

"Hawk, it's been too damn long," Daniel grinned as he grabbed his cane, struggled to his feet and took the big Indian's hand. He hugged him with his other arm, slapping him on the back. Hawk rewarded his cousin with a rare smile.

"What the hell you doing, getting yourself busted up over there? I have several good broncs that would have gladly done the job right here at home," Hawk ribbed his younger cousin.

"Hawk, this is Talia," Nickolas introduced him to a tiny blonde woman sitting as still as death, looking out of the window.

Hawk, always conscious of his intimidating size, walked over and squatted down in front of her. Resting his forearms on his thighs, he looked her in the face. Jesus Christ, she almost brought him to his knees. She was the most beautiful woman he had ever seen. Just being close to her made the hair on his arms stand up and his blood rise.

"Hello, Talia," he managed. "I am Nickolas' cousin." To his surprise, she turned her face in his direction. She didn't exactly look him in the eyes, but he could see hers. They were an amazing color of flat steely gray. He had never seen anything like them. They were unearthly and dead at the same time – so much so, she almost appeared to be blind. She was so still he could hardly detect her breath.

When he saw Talia turn her face toward his handsome cousin, Nickolas was swamped by powerfully conflicting emotions. Joy that she was showing responsiveness, and jealousy that she had responded to Hawk. Now didn't that just make him feel like an ass?

When Hawk rose and went to help Daniel with his bag, Nickolas took his place squatting down in front of Talia.

"Hey, sweetheart, we've come to take you and Daniel home." He cupped her face, turning it more fully toward him. Her eyes didn't meet his, but he was sure he saw her lips tremble ever so slightly. "I know you're not up to taking care of yourself yet, so we are taking you home to the ranch with us. It's quiet out there with hardly any people, I think you'll like it. We'll have to fly, but not military this time. No choppers, I promise." This was greeted with a slight shuddering of her tiny frame. "I'll be with you all the way, Okay?" He stood, taking her by the hand, and pulled her from her chair. She obediently stood as well.

"Where are her bags?" Hawk asked, as he lifted Daniel's duffel to carry it to the limo.

"She has less than nothing," Nickolas bitterly replied. None of the bouquets he'd sent her remained to break the monotony of the sterile room. The staff must have thought she wouldn't notice if they were gone. It was as if they'd cleared out her room while she was still in it. They saw her as a throw away, waiting to be hauled off like so much garbage. If he had not sent the slacks and sweater for her to wear, he wondered if they would have released her in a hospital gown. Her beautiful platinum hair fell into her face, limp and unkempt. He was suddenly so full of rage, he had to work hard to contain it as he tried unsuccessfully to pull her hair from her face. Ever perceptive, Hawk looked at him questioningly, then reached up and untied the leather thong from his own hair and handed it to his cousin, saying nothing. It was moments like these that Nickolas was reminded of the unexpected kindness of the mostly silent man.

"Thanks," Nickolas said in an emotion roughened voice. He pulled Talia's hair back and tied it out of her face at her nape.

~ CHAPTER TWENTY-ONE ~

"How is she?" Hawk asked as he walked into the living room of the ranch house where Nickolas was brooding in front of the fire. Nickolas noticed he had several strips of leather in his big brown hand.

"She finally fell asleep, thank god. The trip was harder on her than I had hoped. What's with the leather?"

"I am going to teach you how to braid," Hawk replied.

"Braid? What is this, happy crafting hour?" Nickolas wanted to know.

"Your woman has beautiful hair; it would be a shame to have to cut it," Hawk informed him as he pulled up a chair and sat directly across from him.

"I am not about to cut Talia's hair," Nickolas told his cousin in no uncertain terms.

"It's very long," Hawk stated the obvious.

"Yes – so?" Nickolas challenged.

"We are in Wyoming. The wind will tangle it until you have no choice."

"Why would I have her out in the wind in the first place?"

"To take her to see Grandfather," Hawk answered, looking down at the leather he was straightening into three strands. "Hold this end." He handed Nickolas one end where he had fastened three strands together with a knot. "You cross them over each other, each in turn," he said as he demonstrated for Nickolas. "Now you try."

"Why would I take her to see your grandfather?" Nickolas asked. He managed to perfect the technique after the fourth try while Hawk held the other end for him.

"Because she has lost her soul. He is a medicine man, a shaman. He will know how to find it. Now try it with my hair, it is different than leather. You have to divide it into three sections," Hawk said. Turning his back to his cousin, Hawk removed the tie from his long black hair, reached into his hip pocket and handed Nickolas a comb over his broad shoulder.

It was a lot different, Nickolas realized as he struggled with Hawk's hanks of hair. It hung to the middle of his back, rather than to his waist like Talia's. Nickolas suddenly really wanted to get this right so he could fix her hair. She had always been so well groomed, every hair in place. He was sure it would make her feel better if he could fix it for her. Hawk sat still and patient while Nickolas untangled another failed attempt and combed it out to try again.

"Am I interrupting an intimate moment?" Daniel asked from the doorway. "I can leave if the two of you prefer to be alone."

"Fuck off," Nickolas said without rancor.

"You're up late. Having trouble sleeping?" the ever perceptive Hawk asked Daniel, unfazed by his teasing.

"Yeah," Daniel said, losing his smile and sinking down on the couch next to his brother. "It might just be PTSD or some such happy horse shit, but I'm beginning to worry."

"What's up bro?" Nickolas asked, letting Hawk's hair fall down into the big Indian's face in his concern for his brother. It was not like Daniel to want to talk about his time in Iraq.

"First, I really need to know, what's with the hair? Is there something you two need to tell me, something that concerns closets and such?" Daniel said, trying to hide his discomfort behind his ever ready wit.

"Hawk was trying to teach me how to braid Talia's hair. So far I really suck at it," Nickolas answered.

"You really did quite well for your first time. You'll get there," Hawk encouraged while pulling his hair back out of his face and retying it at his nape.

"Now that was definitely TMI! I really didn't need to hear that," Daniel said, putting his hands over his ears in mock horror.

"What's up, coz?" Hawk asked, not fooled by Daniel's humor.

"I hear her screaming in my head," Daniel blurted out.

"Who?" Nickolas and Hawk asked in unison.

"Talia, it never stops. Day and night, I hear her screaming. It started in the hospital, but it's still going on. I would think it was just flashbacks or something, but I've never heard her scream. She never lost it, not even under fire, not once."

"What does she say?" Nickolas wanted to know.

"Nothing, just screams like someone is tearing out her soul."

"How do you know it's her?" Hawk asked.

"It's like when she came to me when I was dying, when she spoke to me through you, Nickolas. At night, when I'm asleep I can see her and everything. There's this bloody body hanging in front of her, and she just won't stop screaming."

"Shit!" Again Nickolas and Hawk spoke in tandem.

"What? Is there a fucking echo in here?" Daniel wanted to know.

"I didn't tell you about Carlton. How did you know?" Nickolas asked his brother.

"I don't know anything other than what I see in that fucking nightmare. Did it really happen?"

"Yes, Carlton, the only casualty, he was skinned alive. He was still alive when she found him. When I walked in he was hanging there, begging her to shoot him in the head. I knocked her out rather than let her try to take on his injuries like she did yours. He was too far gone, she couldn't have saved him, and it would have killed her to try," Nickolas confessed.

"Whoa, you're going to have to back up and take me along here," Hawk informed the brothers.

"It's classified," the brothers answered in tandem.

"Now I'm hearing fucking echoes," Hawk came back at them. "So tell me now and shoot me later, this is really important, and your woman's soul lies in the balance."

Nickolas and Daniel looked at each other, shrugged, and filled their cousin in on all that had happened, including Talia's gifts and training. They knew they could trust him with their lives, had actually done so on numerous occasions. If there was ever a man that could not be broken, it would be Hawk. The information was safe with him.

After they fell silent, Hawk sat quietly for so long they wondered if he would speak. Finally he looked Nickolas in the eye.

"Take another stab at braiding my hair."

"WTF?" Daniel wanted to know.

"We need to take you both to Grandfather first thing tomorrow, and you can bet it'll be windy," the big Indian replied. He pulled the tie out of his hair and turned his back to Nickolas, handing him the comb.

~ Chapter Twenty-Two ~

Nickolas woke up to a sound in Talia's room. It was just barely first light. He was out of bed with a 9mm at full draw when he realized it was Daniel wearing nothing but a pair of sweat pants standing over her.

"Fuck, bro. You scared the shit out of me. What are you doing in here, trying to get yourself shot?" Daniel said nothing.

"Bro?" Nickolas put his gun down and approached him. As he got closer, he could see there were tears streaming down his brother's face as he stood looking down at Talia. He had not seen Daniel cry since he was seven and a horse rolled over him. Not even at their parent's funeral had the man shed a tear, but stood military straight and contained.

"I know where we are now, Nickolas, and it is not good," Daniel finally whispered.

"What?"

"When she came and got me the first time, I was almost gone. I was right at the gate, I could see the light at the end of a long tunnel, and she brought me back. She sank her spirit into my body, took my pain and brought me back. Then, when you came and got me, I was right there, more than ready to cross, and she pulled me back again."

Nickolas could tell his brother was in almost a trance-like state, maybe sleep walking.

"That's where we are now, at the gate. She wants to cross, but I won't let her. I won't let her go, but I don't know how to bring her back, and I don't know how much longer I can hold her."

"Hawk!" Nickolas yelled out to his cousin sleeping down the hall. "We've got a problem here."

Hawk appeared in the doorway like a silent wraith, dressed only in his black boxers. Seeing Daniel standing over Talia, he walked over, stood beside him and ran his hand in front of his cousin's eyes. When Daniel didn't blink, Hawk leaned over and looked into his face.

"You're right, we're in a world of shit, he has spirit eyes."

"Jesus, Hawk, now is no time to talk like a damned Indian. What the fuck are spirit eyes?" Nickolas demanded.

"Eyes of those walking between worlds," Hawk responded.

"He said he was holding Talia at the gate," Nickolas shared.

"Get her up and dressed. I'll get him ready. We're out of time," Hawk instructed as he directed Daniel from the room.

~

The sky was overcast with a low ceiling. As promised, the wind was howling. Figures. They wouldn't be able to fly. The only way they could get to the small homesteader's cabin nestled between two red sandstone ridges was on horseback, Hawk concluded, looking at the sky with a practiced eye.

"Do you think you can ride?" Hawk asked Daniel.

"I may be crazy fucked up here, but it will be a cold day in hell when I can't sit a horse," Daniel replied.

"How about Talia? Does she know how to ride?" Hawk asked Nickolas as he handed the reins of a large bay gelding to Daniel.

"I really haven't the faintest."

"You don't know if your woman can ride?" Hawk said, incredulous. For someone brought up on a ranch, it was hard to fathom.

"It never came up, Okay? She can drop the Taliban with an M-16 at three hundred yards at a dead run, is dead accurate with a 9mm, is hell on wheels with plastic explosives and can kill with a touch, but outside of riding me, I have no fucking idea." Nickolas was clearly down to his last nerve, Hawk observed. The normally unflappable agent was losing it.

Shit!

"Okay, you can double up, I'll outfit the big palomino with a blanket saddle, and you can carry her in front," Hawk decided.

"I can do that," Nickolas assured him, looking down at the woman in his arms with an expression so desperate it nearly broke Hawk's heart. A heart the big breed swore he no longer had.

Hawk returned with two more horses in tow. The big palomino would be able to carry both Nickolas and his woman with ease. For himself, he'd saddled his favorite paint. The gelding was large enough to manage Hawk's two hundred thirty pound frame and still agile enough to negotiate the sandstone cliffs. Hawk pulled on his riding gloves and duster, and reached for Talia.

"You really don't want to touch her," Nickolas reminded him.

"I'm covered up, it should be Okay. Get on, and I'll hand her to you."

Nickolas reached up behind his saddle and removed an Indian blanket tied there. He wrapped Talia up, careful to tuck in all her hair before handing her to his cousin.

"You don't even want the wind to blow her hair across your face, believe me," Nickolas informed him.

"God, she must feel like typhoid Mary," Hawk commiserated.

"Yeah, I'm afraid that about sums it up," Nickolas agreed.

~ CHAPTER TWENTY-THREE ~

It had been a grueling three hour ride, not that spending three hours in the saddle had ever been a hardship for Nickolas. He'd practically grown up on a horse. Watching Hawk leading Daniel's mount up the cliff side in the pouring rain while Daniel slipped in and out of consciousness was killing him. Talia was unresponsive in front of him on his own mount, and every so often he had to lean down to listen for her breath to assure himself she was still alive.

Hawk's paint lost its footing on mud and loose rock, scrambling to get its feet back under itself. Hawk took it in stride, skillfully sitting the horse and shifting his weight in the saddle to give his mount the best advantage. Negotiating the sandstone cliffs was treacherous business under these circumstances, and Nickolas was grateful for his cousin's expert choice of mounts.

He realized these were the three most important people in his life, and he couldn't stand to lose any of them. At the moment they were all at risk for one reason or another. Daniel would follow Talia to the other side before he let go of her, and Hawk would follow Daniel off the cliff before he let him fall to his death.

"Shit."

A loud peal of thunder punctuated his muttered explicative.

Iraq was starting to look like a walk in the park. At least there, he understood the enemy. Now, his brother and woman were both lost in the spirit world where he couldn't reach them. Their best hope was his cousin's crazy grandfather. To get there, they had to negotiate the storm swept cliff upon which they were currently serving active duty as lightning bait.

Suddenly a ghostlike figure appeared ahead in the downpour. As it neared, he recognized Hawk's grandfather, hat pulled low and slicker blowing in the wind. He was mounted on a mustang picking its way along the narrow ridge. When they approached, the apparition simply turned and headed down a nearly imperceptible and treacherous wash in the side of the cliff. Hawk followed suit, leading Daniel.

Crap!

The horses were virtually sitting on their haunches, sliding down the muddy slope. On his own he wouldn't have hesitated, but Talia was on his horse in front of him.

"Okay, baby, you're just going to have to trust me here," he whispered into Talia's ear, directing their mount over the edge. He could feel the big palomino struggling under their combined weight. He held Talia close to his chest and leaned back as far as he could, giving the horse its head. Thunder crashed, and the horse trembled beneath them.

"Easy, Tank, you can do this big fella," he reassured his mount. Hearing Nickolas' soft deep voice, the horse steadied. He'd always had a way with horses. In the past, he had simply taken the skill for granted, but in this moment, he was glad for the connection when the life of the woman he loved lay in the balance.

They all reached the bottom of the draw relatively unscathed. Grandfather led them further down the draw and into a cave created by two sandstone slabs. It was open at either end with plenty of room for all four horses and their riders. Lightning flashed and thunder pealed almost simultaneously as the wind wailed and the downpour increased. The horses shifted nervously. Grandfather said something Nickolas couldn't hear.

"What did he say?" he asked Hawk.

"He said the Wakinyan are frisky today," Hawk answered.

"The what?" Nickolas wanted to know.

"The Wakinyan, Thunder Beings," Hawk translated.

"How the hell did he know we were coming?" Nickolas called back to Hawk.

"He said the Wakinyan told him." When Nickolas looked at him in disbelief, Hawk went on to explain. "The old ones are like that. I don't understand it, but I have learned not to doubt it."

The old man dismounted, went to one side of the cave where dry firewood was stored and started to build a small fire. Hawk got down, helped Daniel off his mount and sat him close to the fire. Nickolas balanced Talia on Tank's back while he got off and lifted her down. She stood quietly beside him. Hawk took the horses to one side, removed their bridles, and put on halters from his saddlebags. He tied them to a large fallen tree in the cave that served well as a hitching post. Taking good care of their mounts was second nature to all of the men, but Nickolas was grateful that Hawk filled in so he could get Talia over to the fire. He'd managed to keep her mostly dry under his slicker, but he could tell she was chilled. Her hair was damp where rain had dripped off the brim of his cowboy hat onto her head. He walked her over to the other side of the fire where she wouldn't brush up against any of the other men, then helped her sit on a rock and wrapped the blanket around her shoulders.

She sat silently, staring straight ahead into the fire. Her unbound hair was in total disarray around her face, tumbling over her shoulders and down her back. God, he was going to have to take a curry comb to it, and even that may not make it through the tangled mass. Unbidden came the memory of Hawk's kindness as he tried to teach Nickolas to braid. He idly wished there had been more time for him to perfect the technique.

As if conjured by his thoughts, the breed silently joined them, sitting to the other side well away from Talia. Nickolas could tell Hawk had strategically placed his big frame to serve as a windbreak for her while giving her space.

The old man threw another stick into the small fire. Light from the blaze shown on his craggy, weathered features and long gray braids. No one spoke. Crackling flames and pouring rain were the only sounds.

Lightning flashed, thunder roared, and Nickolas looked up to see grandfather's milky, cataract covered eyes glowing. Christ, the old man had to be nearly blind.

~

After a long silence, Grandfather leaned forward and looked into Talia's face.

"Her eyes have died," he blatantly stated. "Were they like the light from the stars before she left this world?" he asked Nickolas in heavily accented English.

"Yes," Nickolas answered.

"Can she read into the minds of others?"

"Yes."

"She can heal or take life with a touch?" the old man questioned further.

"Yes," Nickolas whispered, his answer drawing a shocked look from Hawk.

"She is one of the Daughters of the Seven Sisters."

"What sisters?" Nickolas asked.

"I would have he who was my daughter's son translate for me, so I may be free to speak true."

Hawk nodded his willingness, and the old man switched to Lakota.

"The Seven Sisters are known to you as the seven stars of the Pleiadean constellation," Hawk translated as his grandfather spoke. "The Daughters are prophesied to come from these stars. The White Buffalo Calf Woman of the Lakota was said to have been one. They are considered the holiest of the holy. Together with the special human men that are their destined mates, they are to bring back The Way."

"What way?" Nickolas wanted to know.

"The Way of the Good Red Road, where all live as one in harmony with our Earth Mother," Grandfather responded.

"I don't understand," Nickolas confessed.

"First, I must tell you an ancient legend of the Lakota. The people had fallen into greed and war, raiding and killing each other for material possessions and the preferred hunting grounds. One day, two brothers were out hunting when they saw a dust storm in the distance. When they approached, a beautiful woman dressed in white fringed buckskin and a pure white buffalo robe stepped out of the storm. The first brother was overtaken by lust for the woman and approached her to lay with him. She did not reject him but reached out and took him into her arms. A dust storm formed around the couple, shielding them from the second brother's view. When at last the dust settled, the beautiful woman remained, but his brother had become a pile of bones.

'You have killed my brother?' he wailed in grief.

'No, I granted his wish and became his mate. We lived a long and loving life and had many fine children together. Now what would you have of me?' she responded in a voice like rain.

'Whatever you would choose to give me,' the man responded, recognizing her divinity.

'Then take me to your elders. There is much war, imbalance and suffering among you. I have come to help you back onto the Good Red Road.'

"The man took her to his elders, and she gave them the Peace Pipe. She taught them the Pipe Ceremony in which the stem represented the male and the bowl the female. In unity they brought balance and peace. She told the elders that the day would come when her line would dwindle until only one ancestor, a woman, remained to carry the sacred Pipe. The men would have become full of themselves, disregard her teachings and take the Pipe from its sacred genetic line. The sacred genetic line was the very line she had initiated through the children she created with the first brother. Rather than allow a woman to carry the Pipe, these foolish men would take it from her and put it into the hands of a male from another line. This would mark the day that the Pipe was broken. It would become stick and stone with no power, and he who took it from its genetic line would be a charlatan, promoting ill will and war against others with the false authority he gained by taking up the Pipe.

"At this time, the Star People would send down the Seven Daughters to save the people from their folly, but would not again offer the Pipe to humans as they had failed in their sacred duty. Instead, the Seven Daughters of the Seven Sisters would be the bowl and seven chosen human males would be the stem. Together, they would bring back the way to all nations.

"When she had delivered her teaching and the prophecies, she returned to the prairie, lay down and rolled in the dust creating another cloud. When the cloud settled, a white buffalo calf stood where she had been. Then a voice like falling rain spoke, saying to watch for the return of the white buffalo calf. The calf would come when the Pipe had been broken, when women, in their time of power, on their moon, were banished from the sacred Inipi, the sweat lodge, and banned from sitting at the drum. It would speak of the birth of the Seven Sisters on earth.

"This legend is told many ways by many peoples, but this is how it was taught to me."

"These women are to be known by their gifts and starlight eyes. Like the ones of your woman. They are holy women, not to be touched by any other than their true mate. To touch one uninvited is to become so overtaken as to end up a pile of bones like the first brother. Only the men that are their destined mates can claim them and stand with them in the storm they bring to cleanse the earth."

As he finished translating the old man's words, Hawk looked Talia up and down, then scooted farther away from her, giving her wide berth in the wake of his grandfather's teaching. He'd been aware of the woman's magnetism from the first time he had been in her presence and did not doubt the validity of the old man's words. He knew too much and had seen too much to ever doubt the old shaman.

"Your woman walks between worlds now as does your brother that holds her to this earth. The cruelty of imbalanced men, those that have wandered far from the Red Road, has driven them both to the edge where Spirit dances in and out of this life. Without her and without him, one stem and one bowl will be missing from the sacred Pipe. This must not be allowed to happen."

"But if she is my woman, as you say, and I believe she is, how can Daniel be her stem?" Nickolas asked, trying to understand.

Hawk dutifully translated his question.

"Yes, you are her mate. There is another sister, the mate to your brother," Grandfather informed him. "And yet another will come that is the mate to he that was my daughter's son."

Hawk paused his translating in astonishment.

"What did he say, Hawk?" Nickolas wanted to know, puzzled by his cousin's sudden silence.

"That there is another sister for Daniel and one for me," Hawk told him, clearly in shock. Gathering himself, he reached into the pocket of his duster and handed Nickolas a fringed leather pouch. "Give this to my grandfather," he instructed.

"Why?" Nickolas asked, taking the pouch.

"It is tobacco. It is traditional to offer tobacco to the shaman for a healing. Later you can gift him with other things, but for now give him this."

Nickolas handed the pouch across the fire to the old man. Grandfather opened the pouch, sniffed the tobacco and grunted his approval. Closing it back up, he stowed it under his slicker.

"Wasté (wash-tay)," he said, passing his hand palm down in front of his chest.

Nickolas looked to Hawk questioningly.

"It means many things depending on the situation, from 'you are welcome' to 'good trade,' but in this case it indicates he has accepted your offering as worthy and will perform the healing for Daniel and Talia."

~ CHAPTER TWENTY-FOUR ~

"I have one question," Nickolas addressed Hawk once the storm had let up and they were underway again. "Why does your grandfather refer to you as 'he who was my daughter's son?'"

"He knows others will not recognize my name in Lakota and refuses to say it in English."

"Why?"

"He thinks it is demeaning."

"What do you mean demeaning?"

"He finds it insulting that I accept the English translation of my given name rather than expect people to pronounce it in Lakota. The old ones can be stubborn that way."

"What is it in Lakota?"

"Canska. It means Hawk."

"Canska?" Nickolas attempted.

"Yes, exactly," Hawk said, surprised by his cousin's accurate pronunciation.

"No reason to be so surprised, I'm not totally inept. I speak eight languages fluently, though I have to tell you, I would gladly trade any number of them to be able to speak Lakota.

"But you often criticize me for talking like an Indian."

"And you criticize me for acting like an agent. It never occurred to me you didn't know how proud I have always been of what you are."

"I would welcome sharing Lakota with you," Hawk formally responded.

He didn't even know Nickolas was bilingual, much less in command of eight languages. He had spent his entire life assuming his cousin was ashamed of his Lakota heritage. It never occurred to him Nickolas might want to learn to speak Lakota. When they were growing up, Nickolas would often end up in fights defending his younger orphaned cousin from the cruel taunts of classmates. Hawk had come to think of himself as no more than a burden, a source of shame and embarrassment to the dynamic heroic cousin he looked up to. Sometimes you knew someone all your life without ever knowing them at all, Hawk decided.

"Great! You can start my first lesson while you finish teaching me how to braid," Nickolas stated, looking down at Talia's tangled mane.

"Well – Okay, but we're going to have to hide out behind the barn so Daniel doesn't freak," Hawk threw back at him.

"Fine, just remember to bring the smokes, sweetie," Nickolas retorted with an affected lisp.

When they were boys, the cousins used to steal one of the ranch hand's cigarettes and sneak out behind the barn to smoke. Though neither man smoked as adults, it was still a standing joke.

"That's downright scary," Hawk told him.

"What?"

"How well you do that lisp thing," Hawk responded.

"You know the rules, don't ask, don't tell."

"God, that is just wrong!" Hawk shuddered theatrically.

They fell silent as they came over a rise, and the small homesteader's cabin that Grandfather called home came into view. The rain had quit, the sun came out and a double rainbow lit the sky, backdropped by the dark storm clouds in the distance. New spring leaves on the huge old cottonwoods by the house lit up as if glowing from within. Grandfather's old sheepdog mix, Sunka, simply meaning "Dog" in Lakota, pulled his arthritic carcass out from under the porch and limped up to greet them.

The banter with his cousin had distracted him for a while, but now Nickolas' gut clenched. What if this was just a bunch of superstition? What if the old man couldn't help Talia? What if she never got better? What if he lost both his brother and the only woman he had ever truly loved?

"The Lakota see a rainbow as a good omen. I have been coming to this cabin all my life and never seen one here, have you?" Hawk asked conversationally.

How the hell did the man do that? It was almost as if he was as much a mind reader as Talia, the way he knew just when to say what. Hawk had always been a man of few words, yet he had spoken more in the last several days than Nickolas had ever heard from him. Nickolas was aware that Hawk's well timed words were one of the few things keeping him sane at the moment.

They came to a stop in front of the small cabin and dismounted. Hawk took the horses to the barn to unsaddle, feed and water.

Grandfather silently indicated Nickolas should bring Talia and Daniel into the cabin.

When they walked inside, Nickolas was swamped by memories brought up by the tidy interior. As boys, he and Hawk would often come and visit the old man. Sometimes in the summer, they would spend up to a month there, helping him tend the sheep and mend fences. Those had been good times. Grandfather rarely spoke, but he had taught the boys volumes with his actions. Suddenly, Nickolas knew that if anyone could help, this man could. God knows, the finest doctors and psychologists had bombed out.

Using wood stored in an old milk box, Grandfather busied himself starting a fire in the ancient cast iron cook stove. He opened the gingham curtains to let in more light and drew leather pouches of herbs from a cupboard. He poured a tin cup of water (reserved on the wooden counter next to the chipped porcelain sink) down the pump to prime it. Working the handle, he filled an old coffee can with water. He also filled a small galvanized water bucket, refilled the tin cup and set it aside. The coffee can of water was put on the wood stove to heat.

At opposite ends of the scarred wooden table, Nickolas settled his brother and Talia on equally scarred ladder back chairs. He squatted down in front of Talia and gently brushed the hair from her face. Between her diminutive size, tangled hair, oversized flannel shirt and dirty face, she looked like a lost waif.

"She loves you, too, you know."

Nickolas looked at his brother in surprise at his softly spoken words. For the first time in hours, Daniel seemed to be somewhat present. Though his green eyes were distant, they met Nickolas' with steady regard.

"And you love her," Nickolas said with sudden insight.

"Yeah, I love her."

Nickolas' heart sank at his brother's admission.

"She pulled me out of the bowels of hell, she is my angel, my sis. I won't let her leave us bro, not on my watch. Just tell Granddad to get on the fucking stick, I'm dying over here."

"He loves her, but not like you do." Hawk chose that moment to silently glide in the door with an armload of wood. "He will have his own woman soon."

"As will you," Nickolas had to remind him.

"Apparently. I've never known the old man to be wrong." Hawk didn't sound like a man looking forward to the prospect.

Grandfather spoke to Hawk in Lakota. Hawk walked over to the stone fireplace and built a fire. He opened an old chest and pulled out two vintage Pendleton blankets, spreading them out side by side, in front of the hearth with reverent hands. This was followed by a folded bear hide and buffalo robe placed to either side of the blankets. Reaching back into the chest, he withdrew a large, fringed leather pouch and placed it on top of the bear hide. The pouch looked to be ancient, handmade from home tanned leather. An abalone shell and a smaller, equally primitive pouch was added the growing pile.

The water on the stove had started to boil and Grandfather added handfuls of various herbs to the can. Soon, their fragrance filled the air of the cabin while the fire crackled in the hearth.

Grandfather spoke again and Hawk walked back to the table. "It's time. Take her boots off, bring her over and lay her down on the blanket closest to the fire," Hawk instructed his cousin as he moved to help Daniel do the same.

159

Nickolas squatted down in front of Talia, pulled up the bottoms of her jeans and removed her boots. He helped her up and led her to the blanket.

"Here you go, baby, just lay down here by the fire," he encouraged her.

Talia complied, stretching out on her back and gazing absently into the flames. Hawk brought Daniel over, careful to keep him a good distance from Talia, and helped him lay down on the other blanket. Grandfather placed dried herbs from the small pouch into the abalone shell. Taking a small stick from the kindling, he lit it in the fire and set the herbs to blaze. He let them burn a short while and blew them out. The fragrant smell of sage filled the air as smoke rose from the shell.

Folding an old red bandana, he placed it on the floor and put the shell on it. He drew the smoke from the shell to himself with cupped hands as one might wash with water, and brushed it over his shoulders, arms, down his trunk and legs.

He picked up the larger pouch and pulled out a square of red felt. He passed it through the sage smoke and spread it out on the floor in front of him. Drawing out an ancient hide rattle decorated with stained feathers, he ran it through the smoke and placed it on the felt. This was repeated with a clear quartz crystal, a piece of obsidian, an eagle feather and a smaller leather pouch on a long leather strap. The pouch was placed over his head to lay on his chest.

He spoke to Hawk again and Hawk returned to the stove. Reaching into his hip pocket, Hawk pulled out his leather gloves and put one on. He lifted the coffee can with his gloved hand and poured a small amount into two tin cups, ladling some cool water from the bucket by the sink into each one. He returned to the fire with a cup in each hand, passing one to Nickolas.

"Help her drink that, then take off your boots and sit cross legged at the top of her blanket," Hawk instructed as he leaned over Daniel and brought the cup to his cousin's lips. Supporting the back of the younger man's head while he drank, Hawk took up position at Daniel's head.

Grandfather picked up the eagle feather and still smoking abalone shell. He passed the shell over each of them in turn, fanning smoke with the large, white tipped feather. Nickolas noticed Hawk drew the smoke to himself with cupped hands just like the old man had done.

"You've been training with him in this," Nickolas observed.

"Yes, I'm the last of the line," Hawk softly admitted. Nickolas looked at his cousin silently for some time, his laser blue eyes penetrating. He turned his attention back to Talia where she lay unmoving on the blanket in front of him.

Grandfather draped the buffalo robe over Talia and the bear hide over Daniel. Kneeling by the pallets, he took up the rattle, shook it and started chanting. Goose bumps rose on Nickolas' arms at the ancient sound. Soon Hawk joined in and the goose bumps spread up and down Nickolas' entire frame at his cousin's powerful, deep baritone. Everything became surreal and time seemed to stand still. The chanting went on and on as both men swayed, eyes closed, appearing to have entered some form of trance.

Without opening their eyes, both men rose up on their knees and seemed to grab something from thin air, bringing their cupped hands to their mouths. Hawk leaned over Daniel and Grandfather over Talia. With totally synchronized movements, they blew through their cupped hands into their patient's chests.

All hell broke loose. Daniel went into convulsions and Talia began screaming in a man's agonized voice.

"If you have a heart in your god damned chest, blow my fucking head off," the tortured man's plea came from Talia's lips.

"God, its Carlton!" Daniel yelled, thrashing under the bear hide. "They've got Carlton."

"Hawk! What the fuck? Do something!" Nickolas yelled at his cousin while trying to pin Talia's thrashing body under him. She was as strong as any man at the moment. If ever there was a full blown possession, this was it.

Seemingly calm, eyes still closed, Grandfather grabbed in the air again. This time he blew into Nickolas' chest. Talia's agonized screams filled his head from the inside. God! How had Daniel stood this? Nickolas could not imagine.

Grandfather grabbed something invisible just above Talia's chest and started to pull as if drawing out a writhing serpent. The old man's arms shook with the effort as he wrestled with an invisible foe. The room filled with a pack of transparent wolves. The buffalo hide on Talia humped up as if filling with an actual buffalo and hawks flew in through the walls.

Shit!

"Nickolas, when I say, 'Go,' put your mouth over hers and breathe into her like you were giving her mouth to mouth," Hawk calmly instructed while struggling to hold Daniel.

Had his cousin sprouted feathers around his face? Looked a hell of a lot like feathers to Nickolas.

The spirit wolves had taken hold of the serpent, aiding grandfather. They were digging claws into the wood floor, pulling backward, hunching with the effort. Nickolas could see through them to the fire behind. He looked back to Hawk for support only to find him gone. In his place a huge red tailed

162

hawk sat on Daniel's chest, mantled as if protecting its prey. Talia's screams echoed around in his skull and Nickolas was convinced he had gone mad. Idly he wondered if it ran in the family, as Daniel continued to thrash and scream for someone to help Carlton.

A ghostly green light floated out of Talia's mouth, and with a final agonized wail of the damned, flowed into grandfather's chest. The tortured sound issued forth from the old man's mouth until the wolves tore into his chest, retrieving a writhing serpent. Wolves, serpent and wail faded into the ethers as they became a whirlwind that rose through the ceiling and disappeared altogether with a resounding pop. Both Grandfather and Talia fell limp and unmoving.

"Go!" the fucking red tail shouted at Nickolas from its perch on Daniel's chest.

Nickolas covered Talia's cold, unmoving lips with his mouth and blew into her. He could actually feel something leaving him and entering her as the scream blessedly left his head. Relief was short lived, however, as the piercing scream broke from her lips, shattering the air with her agony.

Fuck!

He swept her up into his arms and rocked her, stroking her hair.

"It's Okay, she can move it out now," Hawk reassured him.

Nickolas rocked her until her screams finally subsided to whimpers. Afterwards, he sat perfectly still, his face buried in the hair at the top of her head, not looking up, not moving, eyes squeezed shut.

"You Okay?" Hawk asked Nickolas.

"I am not fucking looking at you again until you lose the god damned feathers," Nickolas growled.

"What feathers?" Hawk asked confused.

Nickolas opened his eyes and looked to find Hawk in all of his human glory, sitting calmly next to Daniel who had pushed himself up on his elbows. Both men looked back at him, deep concern in their expressions.

Then he saw Grandfather lying as still as death, apparently unconscious.

"Hawk?" Nickolas called out, concerned.

"He is just helping Carlton get to the other side. He'll be back," Hawk informed him.

"Shit!"

"Did you really?" Hawk wanted to know.

"Yeah, down both legs," Nickolas assured him as he cradled Talia's sleeping form.

~ CHAPTER TWENTY-FIVE ~

The sweat lodge was located down from the cabin next to the creek. The sun had long since set. Hawk had been tending the huge fire for over three hours in preparation for the Inipi ceremony that would complete the healing for Daniel and Talia. Actually, they all needed the healing ceremony, Hawk thought, as he stirred the fire with his pitchfork and added more logs.

Nickolas watched over Talia and Daniel as they drifted in and out of sleep under the hides. The herbs they had been fed earlier must have been a mild sedative, he thought.

Grandfather, seemingly as spry as ever, steeped more herbs on the wood stove in his coffee can and gathered articles in a blanket to take down to the lodge. He moved to the trusty chest and drew out something wrapped in red cotton cloth. Walking over to Nickolas, he handed it to him.

"Undress her completely, and clothe her in this," the old man instructed in his thick accent before returning to the stove.

Nickolas unwrapped the red cloth to find a handmade dress of blue calico folded up with sprigs of dried sage. It was decorated with red, yellow, black and white ribbons across the front and back bodice just under the square neckline, and trailing down the sides. It was shapeless and floor length with loose, three quarter length sleeves. Though the material was sturdy, it seemed very old, as did the ribbons. Seeing that his brother still slept and that Grandfather was studiously ignoring him, he undressed the sleepy Talia and pulled the garment over her head. She made no protest, dozing off as soon as he was done.

Nickolas almost jumped out of his skin when a weathered brown hand appeared in front of his face, offering a brush that looked suspiciously like something one would use on a horse. He dutifully took it, regarding the tangled mess that was Talia's hair. The old man said something in Lakota.

"Just like a horse tail, start at the bottom and work your way up," Hawk translated from the door. The big Indian was wearing only his black boxers. His hair, hanging loose around his shoulders and flowing down his back, lifted in the slight evening breeze. Sweat glistened on the bronze skin of his muscular chest. Hawk said something to his grandfather in Lakota, picked up the blanket the old man had prepared, turned and disappeared into the night.

Nickolas gently removed the tangles from Talia's beautiful hair as instructed, while Grandfather woke Daniel and helped him strip to his boxers, shedding his own clothes as well. Barrel chested and amazingly toned, the old man walked to the stove, lifted the coffee can and looked back at Nickolas.

"Remove your clothes, then bring her," he said, taking Daniel by the arm and leading him from the cabin. He left the door open for Nickolas to follow.

Nickolas was not unfamiliar with the sweat lodge. He had shared it with Hawk and Grandfather numerous times growing up, and was acquainted with the ceremony and most of the customs surrounding it. Carrying Talia to protect her bare feet, he approached the lodge from the proper side, mindful not to cross between the fire and the door.

When he reached the lodge, he put her down, helped her duck through the low entrance, and directed her to crawl clockwise into the dark interior.

"Aho, mitakuye oyasin," he softly spoke as they entered.

Nickolas settled Talia down beside him on the earthen floor and wrapped an arm around her protectively. Daniel joined them, then grandfather entered, sitting to the immediate right of the door. Soft Lakota words were exchanged between grandfather and Hawk who stood just outside the lodge door. Hawk brought hot glowing stones on a pitchfork from the fire, one at a time, and set them inside the door. Grandfather lifted the lava rocks from the pitchfork with a set of deer antlers. The old man reverently placed each stone into the hole in the center of the lodge. At another softly spoken Lakota exchange, Hawk took the antlers from grandfather and set them outside on the earthen altar mound. He handed in a bucket of creek water, into which grandfather poured the coffee can of herbal tincture. Hawk joined them in the lodge, pulling down the flap and sitting to the left of the door. Only the glow of the stones lit the dark interior. Grandfather reached into a leather pouch and cast dried herbs onto the stones. Fragrant cedar filled the air, causing their eyes to water with the sharp pungent smoke. Taking up a chant, he poured a ladle of water over the rocks. Steam rose and the ceremony began.

~

Talia's first awareness was of the incredible heat. Her every breath labored in and out as the fragrant steam permeated her lungs, warming her from the inside out. She could feel tears on her cheeks and sweat trickling down her back. Grief poured out of her like water from a spring and seemed to pool on the glowing stones in the pit in front of her. She could hear chanting and a man's enraged sobs. The rage seemed to mix on the stones with her grief as water hit the rocks from an unknown source. The steam carried both emotions up and away, leaving only the fragrance of herbs in its wake.

She started to shake uncontrollably as another wave of grief and horror welled up inside of her. This time it was so intense, she was wracked with dry heaves. Large, gentle hands held her hair out of her face and stroked her back. Who was touching her? Didn't he know it would destroy him? All she could do was yield. There was no fight left in her as wave after wave of nausea overwhelmed her until she couldn't breathe.

"It's Okay, baby, just let it go. I've got you, Talia."

Nickolas! Reaching up, she grasped his hand where it held her hair and squeezed in desperation.

She had reached out to him! She gripped the back of his hand with amazing strength and held on tight. Nickolas swayed in relief. She was coming back. God, let her be coming back to him.

When her dry heaves finally subsided, Nickolas held her to him and rocked in time to Grandfather and Hawk's chanting. Years ago, grandfather had taught him to pray in the lodge. Now he prayed like he'd never prayed before. The big agent prayed for his brother and for his woman.

Nickolas Pane had feared little in his life. Once his marriage fell apart, his ex-wife's betrayal left him feeling he had nothing left to lose. When he wasn't busy saving the ranch for his brother and cousin, he dove into his work as an agent, fearlessly risking himself to keep others safe, shielding them with his own body if necessary. Now, as he heard the raging laments that tore from Daniel's chest, holding Talia as grief poured from her in wrenching sobs, he felt deep fear. He realized he had a lot to lose.

Nickolas had never before asked for anything for himself, but he asked now. He prayed for a future, for a life with the four other people in the lodge, promising not to waste a single moment should it be granted.

Eventually, Daniel and Talia stilled. The only sounds were that of Grandfather and Hawk's tireless chanting and the water hissing on the rocks, turning to steam. Finally, even that stilled. Nickolas could hear the crickets, the creek, and a gentle breeze as it toyed with the tarps on the lodge. These were the songs of the night just before dawn, the dawn that would break the dark night of the soul.

Now, Nickolas' prayers were ones of gratitude – gratitude and promises. Never again would he doubt the power of magic. He would do whatever it took to shelter Grandfather as long as the old man drew breath. He would do whatever he could to support Hawk in taking up his place as shaman of his line. He would preserve the ranch so they always had a home and Daniel always had a safe haven to return to. He would, by god, win the heart of his woman and give her all she had missed in life. He would lay open his heart and love her with all that he was.

Hawk threw back the door flap with a powerful arm. The light of the rising sun framed his broad, bronze shoulders and flying black hair. The scene could have come from a thousand years ago; it could have come from tomorrow. Across the ages, it meant the same...The long, dark night had finally ended.

~ CHAPTER TWENTY-SIX ~

Talia regarded Tank with trepidation. The horse turned its monstrous head in her direction where she stood by his side, meeting her suspicious regard with one large, questioning brown eye. She was not tall enough to see over his back.

"Really, Nickolas, I don't think this is going to work," she informed him, stepping back from the horse.

"You rode him with me in order to get here, don't you remember?"

"No, I don't remember anything, but it explains a lot," she responded.

"What does it explain?" Nickolas wanted to know.

"Why my butt feels like it does."

Nickolas looked down at her very shapely ass in jeans and stifled a groan. He tried to restrain himself, he really did. Seemingly of its own accord, his big hand cupped her right cheek with a warm caress. She looked at him over her shoulder but, to his surprise, didn't protest.

What was it about his touch? she wondered, not for the first time. His hands were absolute magic. Even a casual touch made her want him, but when he did something like this, she wished she had enough experience to jump his bones. How was she ever going to bring herself to leave this man to his life and go home to hers? The thought of never feeling his caress, never hearing his deep voice again, broke her heart.

"Here, let me set you up on him and I'll get up behind you. You don't have to know how to ride him on your own," Nickolas assured her.

"Well, that's a relief because I have absolutely no clue how to pull that off."

"So I take it the mystery is solved," Hawk spoke from behind them where he had noiselessly approached.

"What mystery?" Talia asked, unconsciously backing into Nickolas as a shield from the massive Indian.

"The mystery of whether you can ride a horse or not," Hawk answered.

"Talia, you remember meeting my cousin Hawk?" Nickolas asked, secretly pleased with her seeking his protection.

"No, I'm sorry. The last thing I remember is – well, it was on mission," she censored herself, ever conscious of classified information.

"Hawk can be trusted. He knows we were in Iraq," Nickolas assured her.

"What else does he know?" she inquired.

"He knows some about you, Talia. It was necessary," Nickolas told her apologetically.

"Yes, I suppose it's probably for the best," she surprised him by saying. "So, if the cat's already out of the bag, would you both mind leaving me alone with Tank here for a little while?"

Both men looked at each other in confusion and shrugged. The horse had a solid disposition and was well trained. Both Hawk and Nickolas had seen to it. Used predominantly for roping and running cattle, Tank would stop dead in his tracks and stand still the moment his reins hit the ground. Nickolas put the massive beast's reins on the ground in front of him. He and Hawk stepped back a respectful distance and faced each other as if to talk. Both men watched from under the brim of their hats to see what Talia had in mind.

"Okay, Tank, we're going to have to get to know each other. I'm going to need you to help me learn how one rides a horse," she whispered to him, slowly approaching and putting one tiny hand on the white blaze of his broad forehead. He rubbed his head against her hand, demanding a scratch, nearly knocking her off her feet.

Nickolas lunged in her direction protectively, but Hawk caught him by the arm.

"Just let them be, you know he won't hurt her," Hawk advised.

Regaining her balance, Talia put her hand on Tank's warm, golden neck and sank her awareness into the horse. Tank trembled at the intimate contact.

"You're a sensitive, like me!" Talia marveled at Tank's awareness of her probe.

"Well, I'll be damned!" Hawk exclaimed under his breath.

"What?" Nickolas wanted to know.

"She communes."

"What do you mean 'communes'?"

"She communes with animals. Have you ever seen her do this before?" Hawk whispered back.

"I don't even know what the fuck she's doing," Nickolas informed him. "Are you telling me she's some kind of horse whisperer?"

"Watch," Hawk advised.

Talia stepped closer to Tank and, resting her head against his shiny neck, sank her fingers into his long white mane. The horse arched his neck, seeming to wrap himself around her diminutive frame, and rested his head on her back. He closed his eyes, nostrils flaring, taking in her scent. They stood like this for quite some time, large horse and tiny woman, eyes closed, still as a statue, breathing as one. Then, to both men's utter amazement, Talia stepped back slightly and the big palomino lowered his head to her. She reached up, unbuckled Tank's bridle and removed it, then scratched his face where it had been. She turned and walked toward the two men, who were now openly gaping at her, with Tank following directly behind her like a puppy.

"The shoe on his left hind foot is loose. He says I am light enough he thinks it will last, but you may want to see to it when we get home," she said as she passed Nickolas, casually handing him the bridle on her way by.

She walked over to a fallen tree and climbed up on the stump. Tank obligingly sidled up next to it. She was still too short to pull herself onto his back. Nickolas moved to help, but Hawk restrained him again, silently shaking his head. Talia put her hand along Tank's neck and closed her eyes. The big palomino stirred and went down onto one front knee, the other leg stretched out in front of him. Talia put her foot in the stirrup, took hold of the blanket saddle, front and back, and climbed on. The horse carefully regained his feet and walked to the men, ever so cautiously, as if he feared unsettling his precious cargo.

174

"The foot thingies are way too long for me and Tank doesn't like the way they flop around without my feet in them," she informed Nickolas.

"You can't ride like that!" Nickolas protested.

"Like what?" Talia asked.

"Without a bridle," Nickolas stated the obvious.

"Truth be known, Nickolas, I can't ride at all, but Tank is sure he can carry me."

"You put the ball of your feet on the stirrups, turn your toes slightly outward, and distribute your weight between your legs and your seat," Nickolas instructed her as he adjusted the stirrups on the blanket saddle, took her booted foot in one hand and slid it in. "I would feel a lot better if you would use the bridle."

"I have no idea how. It would just get in our way," she patiently informed him.

Grandfather approached with two mustangs already saddled up and said something in Lakota. Nickolas looked to Hawk.

"He says you will need your own mount as Tank will throw his shoe if he carries you both," Hawk translated.

"How does everyone know about my horse's damn loose shoe except me?" Nickolas demanded.

"I know because your woman told us. Grandfather knows because he communes," Hawk told his disgruntled cousin.

"Men that turn into birds, wolves you can see through and fucking horse whisperers, what next?" Nickolas muttered under his breath, drawing a smile from his cousin.

Grandfather spoke again. Nickolas looked to Hawk.

"He said you speak to horses as well, but are just too stubborn to admit it," Hawk translated.

"I suppose you do, too?" Nickolas asked his cousin.

"Yes, but nothing like Grandfather or your woman," Hawk answered as he swung up onto the paint in a smooth, practiced movement.

Daniel approached, already mounted and looking more himself than he had since his return from Iraq. He looked at Talia on the bridle-less Tank and back to Nickolas with a raised eyebrow.

"Don't fucking ask me, I've been in the twilight zone for the last two days," Nickolas snapped at his brother.

~

They had been under way for an hour. Nickolas followed behind Talia so he could watch her closely. At first, Tank had walked like he was foot sore, clearly mindful of his inexperienced rider. But soon, horse and rider relaxed into each other. He could see Talia automatically adjust to accommodate Tank's movements on different terrains, leaning forward when they went uphill and backward on the downhill slopes. She had one hand in his mane, the other resting on her leg. She sat the horse as if she'd been riding all her life as the big palomino followed Grandfather's mustang across the rugged ground.

"How the hell is she doing that?" Nickolas asked, dropping back slightly to ride abreast of Hawk.

"Listen to them with your body," Hawk instructed.

"What?"

"They are as one," Hawk tried to clarify.

Feeling more than a little foolish, Nickolas closed his eyes, reaching out to his woman and horse. Suddenly he was there. They weren't speaking to each other. It was more like they were totally in tune, body to body. Tank would move and Talia would automatically adjust. She had totally turned her body over to the horse, and the horse had turned his will to her. It was the most humbling moment of Nickolas' life. In that instant, he recognized the oneness of all things. He knew, without a doubt, that he and Hawk worked with animals in that same synergistic way. It was what made them the best of the best when it came to everything from training horses to calving heifers. He suspected it also played a part in his uncanny ability to detect danger and protect others. He'd taken it for granted, never giving much thought to what he was really doing, but growing up with Grandfather had taught him more than he had imagined. Yet, as he watched Talia, he recognized true mastery. This small woman was one with the natural world in a way he would probably never understand. She was indeed a treasure, one he intended to shelter and protect with his last breath.

~ CHAPTER TWENTY-SEVEN ~

When they finally crested the ridge leading down to the ranch, Talia caught her breath at the beautiful sight. The ranch proper was large and sprawling, consisting of numerous barns and corrals. A Quonset hut used as a garage for heavy equipment and workshop sat to one side. Next to it, three fuel tanks stood on stilts. Two long bunk houses and a cook house were located close to a stream surrounded by huge cottonwood trees sporting tender springtime leaves. On a slight rise above the other buildings sat the two story ranch house and two smaller, one story houses framed by a beautiful, well-kept yard, yellow rose bushes and massive pine trees. A fenced vegetable garden was in evidence. From where they were, they could see numerous ranch hands busy at various tasks, from herding cattle to moving horses from one pasture to another. Smoke rose from the chimney of the cook house, and the smell of fresh baked bread was on the wind.

Talia, mounted on Tank, stood motionless on the ridge. The wind played with his long white tail and her platinum hair as she took in the ranch in amazement. Nickolas looked at his woman and horse, backdropped by his home, and something settled in him that had never been at peace. She belonged here. She belonged with him on this land, in his keeping. Nothing had ever felt so right.

Talia looked over at Nickolas. His bright blue eyes shown from under the black cowboy hat in bold relief against his sun darkened face. He sat the paint with an ease only years in the saddle could bring. Broad shoulders were covered with a western denim shirt, narrow hips and long legs encased in

Wranglers. His hands, covered in deerskin riding gloves and loosely holding the reins of his mount, were crossed at the wrists, resting on the saddle horn. He was a study in virile, rugged masculinity, ever protective at her side. She almost choked on her love for him. This man was everything to her. She would never be able to forget him.

Their eyes met and held. His were full of some unidentifiable emotion, possessiveness mixed with determination, perhaps? She couldn't tell. He had always been hard for her to read, but never more so than now, when there was so much at risk, when he held her heart in his hands. After searching his eyes, she looked back at the ranch below.

"It's beautiful. How big is it?" Talia asked him.

"Around fifty thousand acres," Nickolas responded softly, never taking his eyes from her.

"My, that must be a lot to manage," she observed.

"Hawk is ranch foreman. There's none better," Nickolas said, tilting his head in his cousin's direction.

"I just do what the boss tells me," Hawk countered at Nickolas' praise. "Nickolas is the one running the show."

"What all do you raise?" she wanted to know.

"Horses, cattle and sheep," Nickolas answered.

"How long has it been in your family?"

"Since the mid-eighteen hundreds," Nickolas informed her. "There's only the three of us left now, all bachelors. If my folks were still alive, you can bet they would be putting the screws to all of us to produce some heirs."

His last statement drew a surprised look from Hawk. He had no idea Nickolas considered him as part of the family line in regards to the inheritance of the ranch.

"You must be getting tired of sitting that horse," Nickolas observed. "Shall we go on in?" Not expecting an answer, he reined his mount and started the descent to the ranch.

When they arrived at the stable, a ranch hand approached them to take their mounts. Nickolas dismounted and immediately went to help Talia down.

"Better I lift you off than have Tank do his bowing trick. We don't want to have the hands thinking you've changed him into a circus pony. The poor horse would never survive the humiliation," he teased as he reached up and took her by the waist.

When he sat her on her feet, her legs buckled. Nickolas subtly steadied her until she found equilibrium. She appreciated his sensitivity. Somehow, he'd figured out that any show of weakness on her part embarrassed her. Left to her own devices, she would have fallen flat on her face.

Nickolas reached into the saddle bag and drew out Tank's halter, putting it on him and successfully keeping his bridle-less state undercover. The ranch hand came over to take the horse to the barn. Again, he had protected her secrets, preventing questions she would not have welcomed. The man was so incredibly smooth, it amazed her.

Upon entering the ranch house, Talia noticed it was cool and dim in comparison to the bright, sunny day outside. The change was welcome after three hours in the hot sun. A grandfather clock struck two from beside the massive stone fireplace in the living room. Nickolas took her straight to the master suite and opened the door a careful crack. Puzzled, Talia watched as he stuck his head in, checking inside before opening it all the way for her to enter. When they both were inside, he quickly closed the door again.

"If they get out, they're hell to catch," Nickolas explained, seeing her questioning look. "The big gray one flailed me to the elbow the last time I tried to nape him and get him back in here."

Suddenly she heard a plaintive meow from under the bed.

"My cats? You brought my cats all the way from Nebraska?"

"Yup, heard about it all the way, too," he said with a wry smile. "Apparently, cats are not fond of flying."

"My things!" she exclaimed, looking around the room. "You brought my things, too?"

He shrugged. What there was of them, he thought to himself, looking at the comb, mirror and brush set on his mother's dark cherry wood vanity. There was a small ivory box that held Talia's hair pins and a tiny jewelry box with a rose painted on top. It held a single pair of pearl stud earrings and nothing else.

"I have your dishes and furnishings boxed up and stored in the Quonset. Your laptop is out on the desk," he assured her.

"What happened to my house?" she wanted to know.

"They turned it back over to Habitat. Because you didn't own it, I couldn't do anything to prevent it. I'm sorry, Talia," he said. She nodded in resignation.

She sat on the floor and the cats jumped into her lap. Picking each up in turn, she hugged them to her as if her heart was breaking, and it was – breaking at the loss of her home, breaking at his unbelievable thoughtfulness and all he had done for her. If not for him, she would most likely be forgotten in some institution, her few things tossed into a garbage bin and her cats in a shelter, awaiting adoption or euthanization, whichever came first.

"I don't know how to thank you," she whispered into the gray cat's fur, but Nickolas heard.

She looked down at the unfamiliar clothes she was wearing: Wranglers, boots and a plaid flannel shirt, all wrinkled and mud stained from the last two days events.

"Where did these clothes come from?" she wanted to know.

"I got them for you in Casper."

"Did you have to dress me?"

"Sometimes."

"I'm so sorry I put you through all of this after you'd already been through so much. You didn't deserve that," she apologized.

"It's you that deserve so much better than the hand dealt you, Talia," he assured her, squatting and gently running his knuckles down the side of her face. "I'm sure you're ready for a nice long soak in a tub to ease your saddle soreness. The bath is right through that door. I've set out some towels, and there are more clothes for you in the dresser and in the closet. I'll meet you out in the front room. When you're ready, we'll go grab a bite at the cook house. Hawk went to tell them to expect us," Nickolas said. Rising to his feet, he left her alone in the room, softly closing the door on his silent departure.

~ CHAPTER TWENTY-EIGHT ~

When Talia entered the front room, Nickolas almost swallowed his tongue. She was rosy and warm from her bath, dressed in a western flannel shirt of soft blue and gray plaid tucked into the waist of tight fitting Lady Wranglers. Her legs, accentuated by the heels of her western riding boots, seemed to go on forever and her ass was the thing of dreams – wet dreams. Her hair was up in a high pony tail that hung to her waist. She was free of makeup. Nickolas had no idea what to get her in that department, which was fine by him. As far as he was concerned, she didn't need any. There was something about seeing her in the western clothing that set a fire deep in his soul. She seemed entirely comfortable in the clothes, like she'd been born to be country.

"Feel better?" he asked, attempting to hide his lust. He didn't know how recovered she was and didn't want to pressure her with his desire.

"Yes, much, thanks to the 'Tired Old Ass Soak' you left out for me," she responded with a smile. Nickolas had found the bath salts on one of his trips and could not resist the name. Surprisingly, the combination of bath salts and essential oils worked exceptionally well to ease sore muscles, so he'd left them on the side of the tub for Talia.

"You look great in those, by the way," he could not help saying.

"In what?"

"Those Wranglers, they seem to be cut well for you," he tried to cover his tracks.

"Yes, they are. I've never had a pair, but they're a great fit. How did you know what size to get?"

"I got the size out of some jeans from your house. I didn't even know there was such a thing as a size one. Once I found some, I just had to guess at what style would work for you."

"Good guess," she complimented.

"Hungry?" he asked, as he stood from the large leather recliner and approached her. He needed to change the subject from her fine ass in the tight fitting jeans, or he was going to jump her.

"Starving. You?" she responded, looking up at him.

"Yeah, starving," he said meaningfully as he reached out, running his hands up and down her arms from shoulders to elbows and back again while searching her eyes.

The moment was potent, the magnetism between them crackling in the air. Just when she was sure he would pull her to him and kiss her, he stepped away.

"I'm sure the cook has managed to wrestle us up some grub by now. Do you want to walk or drive?" he asked as he took her arm and directed her to the door.

"Is it far?"

"No, about five minutes' walk."

"Then let's walk. The less time I spend on my tired old ass, the better," she smiled sheepishly up at him.

"I'll have to see what I can do about that when we get back," he offered with an enigmatic smile.

He walked her into the mud room where he took a small, black, western-cut down vest from a hook and helped her into it. It was clearly designed for a woman and fit perfectly.

"Who's is this?" she questioned.

"Yours. I bought it for you when I got the Wranglers. It's cool up here in the evenings."

"You seem to have thought of everything."

He took her by the upper arms and turned her to face him. "I want you to have everything you need, Talia," he assured her in his warm, deep voice.

"I just feel badly you went to so much trouble." She was clearly uncomfortable with his generosity.

"It is my pleasure to provide for you. I wasn't sure of what you would like and I had no clue about makeup. Next time we go into town, you can pick out your own things."

"I can't imagine needing anything more than what you've already purchased, Nickolas. Your choices are perfect, thank you."

The walk was a great idea, she decided, as she and Nickolas walked arm in arm down the hill to the cook house. The wind had settled and the sound of cattle bawling rode on the gentle breeze. As they approached the cook house, she could see it was well kept, but very old. Painted white with a green metal roof, it sat near the stream that had probably been its original water source. Outhouses sat in back of the long narrow structure, and a root cellar, ice house and meat house were off to the side.

"Do you still use the root cellar?" Talia asked.

"Yes, in the winter we can be snowed in for weeks. Because we're so far out here, we need to have adequate food stores. We also harvest quite a bit from the garden, so it makes more sense than refrigeration."

"How about the ice and meat houses?" she questioned, surprising Nickolas that she knew what the old log structures were. The root cellar was more obvious, having a door that led into an earthen mound.

"We don't harvest ice any more since they finally ran electricity out here, but we still use the meat house to hang game. How did you know what they were?"

"Some of the old homesteads in Nebraska had them. I did research when I used to photograph them and got curious as to what they were for," she responded with a shrug.

"You're a photographer?"

"Yes, I used to enjoy taking pictures of landscapes and wildlife."

"I didn't find any camera equipment in your house."

"I had to sell it during a lean month last year," she quietly confessed.

Damn, he could tell by her meager belongings she was not an extravagant woman, so it was not as if she were irresponsible with her money. A nasty thought began to surface.

"How many missions have you done for the military?"

"Over thirty. Why?"

"I notice you aren't beating feet over to the corral to break him yourself, Alex," Wow defended.

"Hel….I mean heck no, Hawk saves me for the tough ones," Alex bragged. Hawk rolled his eyes expressively.

"More like saves you for the light work, you mean. Your old bones are so fu.. so darn brittle, if that bronc threw you, we'd all still be looking for the pieces," Wow informed the older hand.

Talia let the light hearted banter flow around her as Loretta brought in dish after dish of food and set them on the table. She was amazed at how easy it was to be in the presence of the men. While crowds usually stressed her, there was something about the earthy, grounded men at the table that soothed instead. If she concentrated, she was sure she could hear their thoughts, but was not bombarded with them as was the usual case. It was the most normal she'd ever felt, and she welcomed it. Looking up at Nickolas, she found him watching her closely.

"How're you doing?" he asked, remembering how larger groups were usually difficult.

"Really good. I find the company easy to be with," she assured him.

"These men are some of the best - solid, honest, salt of the earth. I'm glad you're comfortable with them. Just don't get too comfortable," he warned.

"What do you mean too comfortable?" Talia asked.

"I find I don't like other men around you," he responded honestly, confusion clear in his tone.

Dinner was down-home and delicious. Pot roast, mashed potatoes, gravy, green beans, beets and home baked dinner rolls graced the table. After the feast, Loretta brought out fresh baked apple pie and coffee. Conversation continued around the table over coffee as Talia relaxed with the cup of tea Loretta had brought her when she turned down the stronger brew. When Loretta came out and started gathering plates, Talia stood up to help.

"Where are you going?" Nickolas demanded, taking her hand in a surprisingly possessive gesture.

"To help clear the table," Talia answered, somewhat perplexed.

"You don't want to run the risk of brushing up against someone, now do you?"

"Of course not, but I do want to be useful. I know how to be careful."

"There will be plenty of time to be useful after you've had time to recuperate. Sit with me and relax for now, and I promise to put you to work later," Nickolas teased to take the sting out of his domineering tone.

With penetrating blue eyes, Hawk watched Nickolas' proprietary behavior towards his woman. Seeing them together made something fall into place that he couldn't quite describe.

Talia's transformation was nothing short of miraculous. Two days before, she had been a childlike wraith with vacant gray eyes. Now, she was a vibrant, powerful woman with diamond eyes and an aura that nearly blinded him. The western clothing suited her in a strange way he would have never expected, and the ranch seemed to wrap itself around her, claiming her as its own. When Hawk looked down the table at Daniel, he saw him watching the couple as well. Daniel, feeling Hawk's watchful regard, met his eyes, and a knowing of the rightness of things passed between them.

The sun had just set behind the red cliffs, and the sky was on fire with the most magnificent sunset she'd ever seen as Nickolas walked her back up the hill to the ranch house. Thunder rumbled in the distance and lightning lit the dark, gathering clouds.

"Looks like we're in for more rain," Nickolas observed. "The lightning storms can be fierce out here. We'd best shake a leg." No sooner were the words out of his mouth than a bolt struck one of the taller cottonwoods by the cook house. The sound was deafening, followed by the crash of a giant, severed limb as it hit the ground not fifty yards down the hill behind them.

"You must be a prophet," she giggled as he grabbed her hand, hauling her the rest of the way up the hill and into the house at a dead run.

~ CHAPTER TWENTY-NINE ~

No sooner had they gotten inside than the lights flickered and went out. The entire ranch was suddenly shrouded in darkness as the last of the light faded from the sunset. Lightning flashed again and Talia was confronted with the shadowy coats on hooks in the mud room. She was suddenly transported into the one room shack with a man's ravaged body hanging in front of her, dripping blood. She whimpered, shaking uncontrollably, then turned and bolted out into the raging storm. Nickolas dashed after her, swept her up in one powerful arm and ran back inside. She shook and sobbed in his arms, struggling violently as they reentered the mud room.

"Baby, what is it? You can't go out in this. You'll be hit by lightning," Nickolas tried to explain, but she was inconsolable. He took her into the living room and sat down on the couch with her in his lap. With one strong arm wrapped firmly around her waist and the other at the back of her head, he held her face into his chest, rocking her as she cried. She put one small hand over his heart, her sweet scent surrounding him. Touching her had its normal devastating effect on the big man. To his utter shame, he couldn't even hold her in her distress without getting a raging hard on. He could feel it swelling against her soft bottom and knew it wouldn't be long before she felt it, too.

Nickolas heard the mud room door open as Hawk and Daniel came in out of the storm. There was rustling as they shed wet slickers and the rubber boots they wore over their cowboy boots. The kitchen door opened, and the two men silently glided inside.

"What's wrong?" the ever perceptive Hawk asked Nickolas when he saw him sitting with Talia in the shadowed living room.

"I don't know," Nickolas confessed. "She was fine, then we were in the mud room when the lights went out, she panicked and ran out into the storm. She's been inconsolable ever since."

Hawk squatted down in front of her as Daniel lit a kerosene lantern on the coffee table. Looking into her haunted eyes, he opened his senses. He let her fear and deep conflict wash over him. Then he looked at her aura. "She is in the past," he informed Nickolas.

"What the hell do you mean, in the fucking past?" Nickolas demanded. He held Talia closer to his chest, territorial jealousy washing over him at Hawk's closeness to Talia. To his shame, he'd all but snarled at his cousin's approach. God, he had to get hold of himself.

"When part of a person's soul has been brought back from being frozen in the past, it needs to process out the trauma in order to fully rejoin them. You may know this as 'flashbacks.' The difference is that, in PTSD, the person relives the trauma repeatedly. Until the severed part of the soul is returned, the person is unable to heal."

"Yeah, don't I just know all the fuck about that," Daniel stated.

"Do we need to take her back to Grandfather?" Nickolas wanted to know.

"I don't think so. She has her soul back and just needs support while she moves through the return of her memories," Hawk said as he stood, stepping back from the beautiful woman in his cousin's arms. Could another ever affect him like she did, Hawk wondered. God help him if he was even more susceptible to his own woman from the stars.

"If it helps to know, I can already I tell the difference in how I feel," Daniel said. "Before, certain things would consistently trigger me. I would be transported back and relive the shit again and again. Now, it's more like I get triggered once, relive it and get over it. The same thing doesn't trigger me the next time."

"Yes, that does help, thank you Daniel," Talia shocked the three men by responding. She nestled back into Nickolas' chest and closed her eyes, her weeping having settled into an occasional hiccup. "Who was he?" she asked quietly, eyes still closed.

"Who?" all three men said at once.

"The man hanging with no skin," she clarified. The men looked at each other helplessly.

"That was Carlton, our only causality. You saved all the rest of us, Talia," Daniel finally answered.

"He was still alive?" she wanted to know.

"Yes," Nickolas replied softly.

"He asked me to kill him."

"Yes," Nickolas confirmed.

"Did I?" she asked so softly they could hardly hear her.

"No, baby, no, you didn't. He died in transport," Nickolas assured her.

"I should have killed him," she shocked the men by saying.

"What?" Nickolas was sure he had not heard her right.

"I was too weak. He was in agony, and I couldn't save him. I should have helped him cross, taken him out of his suffering. He begged me to, and I was too weak. I failed him. I stood with him right there at the gate, I had a gun in my hands and I failed him."

"A man's time is between him and the creator. It was never your responsibility, Talia," Hawk told her softly. "It was up to him to let go and reenter the mystery." The big breed turned and left the room.

Hawk returned a short time later with an armload of firewood and built a fire in the hearth while Daniel poured them all a glass of brandy. The men sat in companionable silence, sipping their drinks and watching the flames, lending their unspoken support as the storm built in power, and rain pounded against the windows. The storm raged outside, but for the first time in her life, she was inside, protected and comforted by three giant men she could never repay nor ever forget. She looked up at Nickolas, her diamond eyes sparkling in the firelight, just as he looked down at her in his arms. A small, reassuring smile ghosted across his sensual mouth, and her love for him took her breath away.

After the brandy was gone, Daniel and Hawk excused themselves and went to bed. Nickolas seemed content to hold her in his arms while the fire died to embers. Talia was equally content to nestle against his warmth, the solid rhythm of his heart soothing where her face rested against his big chest.

When the room started to take on a chill, Nickolas stood and carried her into the master and sat her on the bed. He took a gown from the dresser and handed it to her before going into the bathroom. She changed and was sitting on the bed when he reentered the room. She took her turn in the bathroom, returning to the bedroom to find him lighting a kerosene lantern on the night stand. He'd taken off his shirt and boots and stood wearing only his jeans, partially unbuttoned and riding low on his narrow hips.

God, the man was enough to make her mouth water. His broad shoulders cast a massive shadow on the wall in the flickering flame of the lantern. He turned when he heard her come in and looked at her silently, ice blue eyes searching hers, expression unreadable. The growing bulge in his jeans, however, spoke loud and clear.

He reached one broad hand out to her, and she took it without hesitation. A tremor racked his frame at the simple contact. Closing his eyes, he took a deep, steadying breath, led her to the bed and tucked her in, kissing her on the forehead. He turned to go to his room.

"Nickolas?"

"Yes, baby?"

"Please don't leave me alone."

"I won't leave you. I'll be right over here."

"Nickolas?"

"What, Talia?"

"Would you please hold me?"

He stood still and silent, long enough that she was sure he would refuse. He returned to her bed, laying on top of the covers with his jeans still on and gathered her into his arms, holding her close.

Heat radiated off his big body, warming her. She could feel his desire washing over her in scalding waves, but he made no move to take her. She knew she was being unfair, that he was making every effort to get over his addiction to her, but she just had to have one more night in his arms. Tomorrow she would do what she knew was the right thing, but, god forgive her, she just had to have tonight.

~ CHAPTER THIRTY ~

"Just what in the hell do you think you're doing?" Nickolas asked in a soft voice, all the more dangerous for its restraint. He stood in the doorway of the master, one broad shoulder leaned up against the jam, cowboy boots crossed at the ankles, arms across his muscular chest. He had just come back from driving cattle from one pasture to the next. The sun was hardly up, and he'd returned to see if Talia was ready to go to the cookhouse for breakfast. Instead he found her still in her night gown with an open suitcase on the freshly made bed.

"Just what it looks like. I'm packing," Talia responded without looking up from her task.

"And where are you planning on going?" he demanded quietly.

"Back to my life so you can get on with yours. I'm not an invalid any more, Nickolas. There's no longer a reason for me to impose on your hospitality. I'll reimburse you for all the clothes and expenses you incurred as soon as I get on my feet."

Nickolas squeezed his eyes shut, pinching the bridge of his nose between thumb and forefinger in an effort to rein in his temper.

"I don't see you as an imposition and I don't want to be reimbursed, Talia," he finally managed in a fairly reasonable tone.

Her hands stilled in the process of folding a soft T-shirt. She looked up into his face and found it unreadable. Agent Pane was alive and well.

"Nickolas, I owe you my life. I refuse to repay you by destroying yours. Dr. Wilkinson told me that you would move through the addiction much quicker if I'm not around. He assured me at the start of our mission that you have the strength of character to move beyond this where others have failed."

"So that's what you think you are to me, an addiction?" he wanted to know.

"What else? You know what I am, and you know my track record."

"What am I to you, Talia?" he asked, straightening up and moving closer to her. He crowded her between the big master where her suitcase lay open, and his big masterful body where his heart lay open and bleeding.

"That's not the point," she evaded.

"Oh, but it's exactly the point. Yes, I know your track record, as you call it, and I also know I was your first lover. Where does that leave you?"

She dropped her gaze to the suitcase and continued folding the T-shirt. It was incredibly soft, clearly high quality. She could tell he'd put a lot of thought into all he'd purchased for her. Fighting tears, she simply shook her head, not wanting to let him see her heart was breaking.

"Look at me, Talia," Nickolas demanded.

She shook her head, not looking up. She wouldn't even meet his eyes. It broke him. He swept the suitcase from the bed with one powerful arm. It sailed across the room and crashed against the opposite wall, causing her to flinch.

"I won't let you walk away from me, not now, not ever. Do you hear me?"

"And I won't spend the rest of my life being your debilitating addiction. You deserve better than that."

"You're not my damned addiction," he countered.

"Nickolas, think. All the signs are there, you're jealous, possessive and controlling. You protect me like a dragon hording its treasure. Those are signs of addiction."

"I'll tell you what you are to me, woman, you're my god damned wife, legal and binding," he shouted, grabbing her by both wrists and pulling her to him.

"Wife?" She couldn't have heard him right.

"Wife. We were declared common law."

"Why?"

"So I could gain custody of you and keep you from spending the rest of your life vegging away in some damned institution. So I could take care of you, so I could bring you home where you, by fucking god, belong," he raged.

"Why would you tie yourself to me like that? Dr. Wilkinson must have told you I probably wouldn't ever recover. Did you feel like you owed me because of Daniel?"

"I can never repay you for what you did for Daniel."

"We can get this fixed, we can get an annulment," she pleaded.

"I tied you to me because that's exactly where I want you. There will be no damned annulment!" he roared, lifting and all but throwing her on the bed. Covering her with his massive frame, he held both her hands over her head in one powerful fist, wrapped the other in her braid at the back of her neck to control her, and ravaged her mouth.

She whimpered and squirmed underneath him, driving him into a frenzy of lust. He would have her. He, by god, would make her his, the only way he knew how.

Releasing her braid, he ripped her gown from her body, spilling out her gorgeous breasts. Damn, he'd missed them. The sight of their perfection stole his breath. Cupping one pink tipped globe, he lowered his mouth to the other, suckling as if his life depended on it while she continued to struggle.

"Please," she begged. If he kept this up, she would never be able to leave him. His mouth sent electrical shocks directly to her womb. She was drenched with her desire for him - only him. She had not lied when she said there would be no other. Suddenly his hand found her wet mound and two thick fingers entered her in a brutal thrust, withdrew and thrust in again, even deeper. She arched off the bed. He released her wrists, slid down her body and latched his mouth onto her while still thrusting his fingers in and out.

His heart soared when she opened her legs for him and arched up to meet his mouth and hand. She wanted him, she still wanted him. If he could win her body, her heart would follow, he was sure of it. It was just the kind of woman she was, pure and sincere. Sex could never be a casual act for her. He could feel her body winding tighter, soaring higher. Her legs began to tremble and she was creaming copiously. She no longer fought him, but pulled his head to her as her hips thrust helplessly and her whimpers of protest turned to those of passion. He added a third finger. Her body arched like a bow, and she screamed her orgasm while he delved deeply into her hot depths, held her clitoris between his front teeth and flicked it with his tongue.

She was still shuddering her release when he unzipped his pants, releasing his engorged cock and mounted her. Pressing the swollen head against her entrance, he froze, supporting himself on his massive arms.

"Tell me you want me inside you, Talia," he groaned. "I need to hear you say you want my cock in you." He, by god, *would not* take her against her will.

"I want you in me, Nickolas, only you." The moment was raw, demanding brutal honesty. She gave it to him, first in her words, then in her screaming response when another orgasm crashed over her. With one driving thrust, he had buried himself deeper than he had ever been before, pushing her over the edge.

"Ah, Jesus, baby, I would die for this, I would die for you," he moaned. "Say it again," he demanded, slowly pulling out of her, inch by agonizing, rock hard inch.

She cried out, "I want your cock in me. I want you deep, and I want you now." Wrapping her legs around his jean clad hips, she sank her nails into his back through his shirt and her teeth into the cords of his neck next to his collar.

"Oh, god, woman, oh, god!" His control shattered and he went wild, pounding into her again and again. He reared back onto the heels of his boots, forced her to straddle his legs and pulled her up on to his cock by her hips. He thrust deep and hard; still, he wanted more. "Sit up, wrap your legs around my waist. I want in deeper," he demanded.

He demanded and she complied. She could feel each powerful plunge bludgeoning her cervix as if to demand entrance into her very womb. Her bundle of nerves ground against his pelvis with every thrust. In this position, her entire body weight was committed to their joining. He had total control. Due to his substantial size, he had the power to cause her harm with his possession, but instead he supported her hips with his big hands and danced the edge of pleasure/pain with masterful precision.

"I'm going to come again! God, Nickolas, you're going to make me come again!" she wailed. Looking directly into his screaming blue eyes, her own, molten silver, were full of tears. Then she threw back her head, arched her back and impaled herself on him, shattering in ecstasy.

He exploded. Pulse after scalding pulse pumped into her spasming depths while his heart poured out of his chest and into hers.

He didn't have to ask if he'd hurt her. Hell, there was no way he had not. He was very large – everywhere, while she was delicate and small. He was totally buried in her, could feel her muscles quivering in protest. Suddenly, to his utter amazement, she came again, convulsing around him.

"Oh, god, you are so deep inside me," she groaned as another endless orgasm shook her frame, milking yet another from him.

Finally they lay on their sides, spent but still joined. His arms were wrapped around her. Her leg was thrown over his hip, one small hand resting on his shirt over his heart. They couldn't break eye contact. He still had his fucking boots on, for Christ's sake.

"You admitted yourself you don't know squat about men," he finally spoke.

"Yes, I did."

"You cited my behaviors: jealousy, possessiveness, protectiveness and controlling, as symptoms of addiction."

"Yes," she agreed.

He reached and covered her hand with his where it rested over his heart. "You might as well stop my heart right now."

"Why? Why would you say such a thing?" she asked, alarmed, trying to pull her hand away. He held fast, refusing release it.

"Those obnoxious tendencies you attributed to me may be signs of addiction, but they're also signs of a man in love." His brow furrowed. "Stopping my heart would be a hell of a lot more merciful than tearing it out. If you leave me, Talia, you will tear my heart right out of my chest. Please, baby, just give me some time to earn your love. Give me some time. Give us a chance, Talia, before you throw me away."

She looked up at him with starlit eyes for the longest time before giving him a single nod and resting her face against his chest. Soon she was asleep, spent from their passion and exhausted from the emotional storm.

What did that mean, he wondered. A day? A week? How long did he have to find the gentleness in him that this beautiful, fragile woman deserved? So far, he'd been so overcome by his lust for her; he had ravaged and manhandled her at every turn. He took in her ruined gown, the upended suitcase and her clothes strewn across the room. Looking down at her, he saw that her hand still rested over his heart in her sleep. He ran his thumb over the bruises on her delicate wrist where he had grabbed her in his desperation, and closed his eyes in agonized shame.

~ CHAPTER THIRTY-ONE ~

"What ya doing bro?" Daniel asked Nickolas when he found him sitting in the study at their father's old desk. The safe was open and a set of white velvet boxes were in front of him on the dark wood surface. He was rolling a ring around between his big thumb and forefinger, looking off into the distance broodingly.

"I'm afraid I am going to blow it, Daniel, afraid I'm going to drive her away," Nickolas confessed. He gently put his mother's wedding ring down next to its box. Putting his elbows on the desk, he covered his face with his hands.

Daniel pulled up a wooden chair and sat on it backwards, arms over the back, and regarded his older brother in concern. He had never seen him like this. Betrayed, yes, pissed as hell, yes, defeated even, but not in such desperate despair.

"In all the years I was married to Nancy, I never once lost my cool. Even when I walked in on her and found her in bed with that bilbo, I just turned around and walked away. I never manhandled her or yelled at her. I never threw things or tore her clothes and I was unerringly gentle with her in bed. I know how we're built, Daniel, I know to be careful."

"What's happened?" Daniel asked in growing alarm. Surely his brother hadn't hurt the diminutive, delicate Talia. God, if he had, he didn't trust what he himself might do. "Have you hurt her?"

"She says no. But, god, I can't control myself around her. I've never wanted someone like I want her, and when she was trying to leave me, I swear I would have pinned her down and hog tied her to my bed to keep her with me."

"She was trying to leave?"

"Yes. She thinks I'm addicted to her and that she's a charity case here. She says she wants me to be free of her to live my life. I have no fucking life without her!"

"What does she mean addicted?"

"It's the 'can't-touch-or-want-forever' effect she has on men. I understand that. But I wanted her long before I ever touched her. I love her, but I can't seem to control myself around her. When I found her packing her bags, I threw the fucking suitcase across the room. It had to have terrified her. The more I'm afraid of losing her, the more volatile I get, the less control I have when I need it the most. I'm rough with her in bed. I just know I'm going to fucking blow this, and there has never been anything more important to me in my damned miserable life."

For the normally stoic, shut down Nickolas, that was a virtual dissertation. Daniel could see his brother was in a butt load of pain.

"Have you tried talking to her about it?" he ventured.

"When I'm not forcing her around, bruising her wrists, ripping off her gown or barking orders, you mean?"

"All that?"

"Yeah."

"Shit!"

"Yeah."

"You want me to take her into town?"

"NO! I don't want you to take her into fucking town!"

"Do you think she is safe here, bro?"

"Yes, I can *by god* control this thing. I have to. She has agreed to give us time. I don't want to blow it."

"Damn, bro, I've never seen you like this."

"No fucking shit."

"What's with the ring?" Daniel asked, indicating their mother's wedding band with his chin.

"I want to ask her to marry me. I know we're common law, but she deserves the real deal. I'm just afraid it may be too soon. I want to get her a ring, but she hates to be around people. Taking her shopping is not an option. I just don't know what the fuck to do."

"Why don't you show her the ranch?"

"What?"

"Take her out riding. Show her the Hole in the Wall. Stay over at one of the nicer line shacks or the ol' homestead. Do easy stuff for a while. Let her get to know you when you aren't both under fire."

"Great idea! You're brilliant! Thanks Daniel," Nickolas exclaimed as he jumped up from the desk and headed out. Pausing at the door, "Grandfather said there is a sister for you."

"Yeah, I heard that. You're making it look like so much fun, I can hardly wait."

"Well, if I can ever do the same for you, well – I'll be there for you, bro." Then he was gone.

Daniel picked up the rings, replaced them in their velvet boxes and relocked them in the safe, shaking his head. Man, Nickolas had it bad. But then, a woman like Talia had that effect on a guy. And there was supposed to be one out there somewhere for him? He couldn't even imagine another like her.

~ Chapter Thirty-Two ~

"Hey coz, can I impose on you for a favor?" Nickolas asked Hawk when he finally located him. Hawk was in the Quonset hut, wrenching on the engine of one of the ranch's older pickups.

"Sure, what's up?" Hawk responded, wiping his hands on a grease rag and giving Nickolas his full attention. Hawk had a way about him, grounded and solid. When he gave his attention, it was as if nothing else mattered but what you had to say. Nickolas had always appreciated that about the man, but never more so than now.

"I know you're busy and I'd send Daniel, but, with all he's been through, I'm not comfortable with him flying alone yet. I need someone to fly the Cessna into town and pick up some stuff, then fly right back out before dark. It will require a few stops in town, but except for one item, the stuff isn't bulky. Weight won't be a problem on the flight back."

"Let me wash up, give me your list, and I'm out of here."

No questions asked. That was Hawk.

"I'm going to order the stuff online, make some calls and have it ready for you to pick up. Most of it's probably at Sam's, but some at the outfitters and one stop at a jewelry store. Call me when you hit the ground, and I'll let you know where I found all of it."

"You got it," Hawk said on his way out the door.

"Hawk?"

"Yeah?"

"Thanks, man. This is really important to me."

"Never a problem."

~

That evening the sun was setting and Nickolas had just walked Talia back from the cook house. The sound of the Cessna's engine could be heard as it banked over the red cliffs and made a pass at the dirt strip to chase the sheep off before landing. Man, but that boy could fly, Nickolas thought, as he always did when watching Hawk handle the craft. Natural born aviator, his name did suit.

"Hawk is back from town with supplies. I'm going to take the Rover down, help him unload some stuff, and bring him to the ranch house. I won't be long," he said, leaning down to kiss Talia on the forehead. He took his denim jacket from a peg in the mudroom on his way out. She heard the screen door slam behind him. His sudden departure was a little odd as he hadn't let her out of his sight all day. He'd been by her side, ever watchful since they'd gotten up from napping. It was as if he was afraid she would disappear if he took his eyes off of her. She had no idea her trying to leave would have such a negative impact on him. He seemed edgy and wounded, and it broke her heart.

"Nick go to pick up Hawk?" Daniel asked from so close behind her, she nearly jumped out of her skin. "Sorry, sis, didn't mean to scare you."

"For big guys, all three of you can sure sneak up on a person. Why did you call me that?"

"What? Sis?"

"Yes."

"You're my brother's heart. That makes you my sister in my book," Daniel stated quietly, searching her eyes with his. After a time he added, "He is one tough son of a bitch, but you have the power to destroy him."

"I'm fully aware that what I am can destroy him," she stated, hanging her head.

"No, it's not that. He can manage what you are. Like I said, he's one tough son of a bitch. If you walk away, you walk away with his heart – *that* will destroy him," Daniel said quietly. He silently looked into her startled eyes. Turning on his heel, he went into his own room and softly closed the door behind him. In the wake of his powerful statement, Talia was left alone and stunned in the fading light of the living room.

~

Hawk had just climbed out of the Cessna when Nickolas pulled up in a cloud of dust.

"Looks like a whole lot o' courtin' going on," the big Indian addressed Nickolas with a rare smile. Reaching in the front pocket of his western dress shirt, Hawk pulled out a velvet box and handed it to him.

"Yeah, I'll do whatever it takes. She deserves so much better than what I have managed so far," Nickolas said. He opened the box and looked at the diamond ring inside.

"Quite a piece," Hawk observed. "How did you know what size?"

"I remembered Mom wore a 6. I pulled out her rings this morning and took a look at them, then just guessed. I can always get it sized if it doesn't fit, or exchanged if she doesn't like it. What do you think?" he asked, holding the box out for Hawk's examination.

"Quite a piece," he repeated. "She is a small lady but with a large spirit. I think it suits her. She can manage it well."

"This saddle is a beaut," Hawk continued, as he unloaded it from the side door of the Cessna. "Do you think she will actually use the bridle?"

"I can only hope. Otherwise the hands are going to start talking," Nickolas chuckled, then sobered. "Hawk, I want to gift Talia with a horse. Do we have something suitable or do we need to pick one up?"

"I just finished with this little palomino mare," Hawk replied after giving the question some thought. "She is out of Tank's mom. She took well to training, only managed to dump me once. Has spirit, and I normally wouldn't suggest her for a beginner, but your woman – has a good way. The mare is as smooth gaited as a rocking chair, sure footed and courageous. She will do right by Talia."

"Did you have your heart set on her?"

"Nah, she's too small to haul my oversized ass around. I really hadn't decided what to do with her yet. She's agile and would make a great roping pony, but it would be a shame to waste her on one of the grizzly ol' hands. She's a beauty. She and your woman will suit."

"Would you mind fitting Talia's new bridle and saddle to the little mare tonight, then put her in the main corral and meet us

216

here tomorrow morning after breakfast? I would like you to be there to introduce them."

"I'd consider it an honor," Hawk responded before throwing the heavy saddle over one huge arm and walking toward the Rover with his silent, loose gaited stride.

The men loaded the rest of the packages into the Rover and drove to the barn where they dropped off the saddle, matching saddle bags and bridle before heading to the ranch house.

"Nickolas?"

"Yes."

"I've been thinking. If you give me that new saddle and throw in the saddle bags, I'll marry you. You can keep the ring and won't even have to kiss me first," Hawk teased. Nickolas almost drove off the dirt road while punching his cousin in the shoulder. Somehow the big man always knew just the right thing to say. Both were still laughing and exchanging playful punches and insults when they walked into the ranch house. Talia was sitting on the couch in the dark in front of a cold fireplace.

"Talia, baby, you Okay?" Nickolas asked in concern, rushing to her and squatting down in front of her, only to be greeted by a venomous hiss and flashing claws.

"Shit! You released the beast! We're all doomed!" he exclaimed in mock horror as he jumped to his feet, well away from the enraged gray tom on Talia's lap.

"Nickolas! You're home. Sorry, I drifted off," she responded sleepily.

"You need my help with that there wild cat, or can I safely retire?" Hawk asked from the shadows.

"Which one?" Nickolas threw over his shoulder.

"The gray one. You're on your own with the blonde," was the chuckled response on the way to his room. He quietly closed the solid pine door behind him.

"Do you want me to light a fire, or are you ready for bed?" Nickolas asked Talia, still giving the enraged tom wide berth.

"Actually, a fire would be nice."

"Deal. You put mister hiss back in his room, and I'll light the fire and pour us a glass of brandy."

Nickolas left the lights off and lit the fire. He poured a good measure of the rich amber liquor into two crystal snifters. When he returned to the living room, Talia was back on the couch in front of the fireplace. He sat down next to her and handed her one of the glasses, then carefully pulled her under his arm next to his side. They sat in silence for a while, staring into the flames, sipping the brandy.

"Talia?"

"Yes?"

"Are you afraid of me?"

"No. Why would you think I was?"

"You're kidding, right?"

"No."

"I've been a total bastard. I'm sorry."

She looked up at him, starlit eyes shining in the firelight. He reached out and stroked her hair, drew her to his chest and kissed the top of her head. Outside of the crackling fire, silence reigned. She amazed him by snuggling deeper into his embrace. They finished their brandy in companionable silence as the fire started to die down.

"Talia?"

"Mmm?"

"I want to take you to bed. Will you share your bed with me?"

"Where have you been sleeping?"

"In the small room off of yours."

"Why?"

"I wanted to be close in case you needed me."

"I mean, why have you not slept with me?"

"I didn't want to take advantage."

"Yes."

"Yes what?"

"Yes, I would love to share *your* bed with you."

"I don't know if I can be a gentleman," he warned.

"Good."

"Good?"

"I don't want a gentleman, Nickolas, I want you."

"I hope that tom is well asleep under the bed, or I may have to call on Hawk after all," he teased. Sweeping her into his arms, he carried her to their room, pushing the door none to gently closed with his boot heel.

He undressed her slowly and reverently, determined to make it good for her this time.

"I was rough with you, are you sore?" he asked, gently cupping her mound through her panties after he removed her jeans. He stood behind her and held her to his chest, one hand on her mound, the other fondling her breast through her lace bra while he delivered open mouthed kisses to her nape.

"Nothing we can't work around," she hedged.

"Have I damaged you, Talia?" he asked in concern.

"No, you're just very large and I'm not very experienced yet."

"Let me see what I have done," he demanded, pulling her panties down and pressing her onto the bed, separating her legs for his inspection. She complied, blushing crimson. He spread her folds with his thumbs and inspected her feminine core, finding it raw and inflamed from his brutal possession that morning. There were fingerprints on her delicate hips and legs from where he'd held her and ravaged her. "Oh baby, I should be shot for doing this to you. How can you even stand the sight of me?" he agonized.

"You could kiss it and make it better," she suggested. Startled, he looked up into her face. "I love it when you put your mouth on me, Nickolas."

"Oh, god, woman!" he groaned. Helpless to do otherwise, he lowered his mouth to her mound and gently ran his tongue over her enflamed slit. She moaned and arched into his mouth. Wearing nothing but her lace bra with her long legs spread wide for him, she was a study in carnal temptation. A temptation he would, by god, resist. He leaned away from her after placing an apologetic openmouthed kiss over her core, removed her bra, stood up and walked away. She pushed up on her elbows and watched him disappear into the master bath in disbelief.

Soon she heard the sound of running water and he returned. He swept her up into his arms and carried her into the bathroom. The tub was filling, steam rising, and she could see the opened bottle of Tired Old Ass Soak Salts sitting on the counter. He gently deposited her into the tub, knelt next to it and took up a washcloth and the bar of French milled soap he'd purchased for her before bringing her home from the military hospital.

"What are you doing, Nickolas?"

"Tending to my woman."

"You've been doing that since we left Iraq."

"I hope to do it for a lifetime," he said, looking down at her with his laser blue eyes while running the warm soapy rag over her slender back.

Nickolas bathed her, rubbed her dry with a thick Egyptian cotton towel and tucked her into bed. Stripping, he joined her and pulled her into his arms, her back flush against his chest, and kissed her on the top of her head.

"Sleep well, baby," he whispered. She snuggled in and immediately complied, the bath and brandy doing its job to perfection.

~ CHAPTER THIRTY-THREE ~

"Wake up, sleepy head, I have plans for you today," Nickolas whispered into her ear, nuzzling her neck from behind.

Talia woke to soft predawn light and rough whiskers, totally wrapped in the warmth of the amazing phenomena that was Nickolas in the morning.

"I hope those plans include sleeping in and making love," she retorted, noting his early morning wood prodding the small of her back.

"Sleeping in, no, making love – possibly later," he answered with a smile in his voice, then shocked her by slapping her bare backside. "Up woman, daylight's a burnin'."

When they arrived at the cookhouse, the sun was just breaking over the red cliffs. The smell of fresh coffee and bacon washed over her as Nickolas opened the screen door and escorted her inside. A huge pile of flap jacks sagged off a large platter in the middle of the table. The ranch hands sat around drinking black coffee, exchanging stories and insults until someone noticed their arrival. Chairs scooted as they all stood, hats in hand.

Silence reigned.

"How you like your eggs, little miss?" Loretta loudly inquired, interrupting the cowboy benediction as she waddled into the dining room, wiping her hands on a well-worn cotton dishcloth.

"Oh, I like them," Talia couldn't resist teasing.

"I mean how do you like 'em cooked?" Loretta clarified.

"That's how I like them best," Talia responded, tongue in cheek.

For thirty seconds you could have heard a pin drop. Then a snort came from the vicinity of Shorty, a chuckle from Mex, followed by a guffaw from Hank. Soon the room was filled with laughter and everyone relaxed into the moment.

"Smart ass," Loretta declared, swatting Talia on the arm with the dishtowel in good natured retaliation.

"Must be the Tired Old Ass Soak perked it back up," Talia responded, smiling up at Nickolas. "Scrambled would be perfect, Loretta, thanks," she added.

Just like that, she had become family to the crew, Nickolas realized in admiration. It was clear she'd done it to put them at ease. In doing so, she'd won their undying devotion. He held out her chair, admiring the ass in question in her form-hugging Lady Wranglers as she took her seat. Damn, but the woman looked good in a pair of jeans.

They had just taken their seats and conversation resumed when Hawk and Daniel came. Hawk met Nickolas' eyes, gave a small affirmative nod, and turned to answer Loretta's question about egg preference. In that moment, Nickolas realized he'd been dead without even knowing it. Dead to the richness of his life and the loving, loyal people in it. The loss of his parents, end of his marriage, and what he still considered murder of his unborn child had all but destroyed him.

Now, sitting in the warmth of the cook house, surrounded by his family and loyal crew with this beautiful woman at his side, his heart was full to overflowing. She had saved his brother's life and brought him back to his. There wasn't anything he wouldn't do for her. Reaching over, he took her small hand where it rested on her lap, laced his fingers through hers and brought it to his mouth, kissing her knuckles. It did not go unremarked by the grizzled hands who carefully hid pleased smiles behind good natured banter.

"You want your usual over-easy or are you going to make a meal out of lady fingers?" Loretta teased as Talia blushed prettily.

When they'd finished breakfast, Nickolas pulled Talia's chair back for her and Hawk stood to leave as well.

"Daniel, Hawk and I are going to show Talia something over at the barn. Want to join us?" Nickolas offered, thinking to include his brother in the surprise.

"Sure, I was going to saddle up and check on the sheep in the high pasture this morning," he responded. "The coyotes were singing from that direction last night, never a good sign."

Nickolas was glad to see Daniel starting to take interest in ranch affairs again, a sure indication his brother was on the mend.

As they approached the barn, Talia noticed there was a horse in the main corral by itself. All three men walked over to the fence with her, watching her closely. She looked from them to the dainty Palomino in the enclosure.

"What happened to him?" she asked in feigned concern.

"Who?" Nickolas asked.

"Tank, someone shrunk him!" she exclaimed, drawing an appreciative laugh from all three men.

"Wrong equipment, Talia, that's a mare," Nickolas teased her back.

"She sure is pretty," Talia said sobering. The little mare had a long, cream colored mane and matching tail so long it nearly brushed the ground. She obviously had been recently groomed. Her golden coat shone in the sun as she pranced around the corral on dainty, high stepping, cream socked feet.

"She's Tank's little sister," Hawk informed her. "They have the same mom. Want to come meet her?"

"Yes, yes I would," Talia enthused, eyes bright, quite taken with the pretty little mare. Nickolas looked on, beaming at her apparent pleasure. He lifted Talia onto the rail so she could hop to the other side while Hawk effortlessly swung his big frame up and over. Nickolas and Daniel remained on the outside of the fence, leaning on the rail with both arms as Hawk and Talia approached the mare. The horse looked at them suspiciously out of the side of one soft brown eye, threw her head, long mane flying, and pranced off a little distance.

"I'll catch her for you," Hawk offered, reaching for a halter hung on the fence post.

"Can I try first?" Talia surprised the men by asking.

"Sure," Hawk responded, leaning back against the fence post, crossing his arms over his chest and settling in to wait in his quiet, patient way.

Talia didn't know what it was about the pretty little horse, but it was suddenly very important to her to make friends on its terms. She slowly walked into the center of the enclosure and stood, not approaching the horse. The horse snorted and stomped her foreleg before prancing off again. Talia did nothing. The mare observed the quiet, small human standing in the center of the pen. She threw her head and trotted off a little further. The human didn't move. What was it about that two-legged with the long mane? the horse wondered, and took a few tentative steps in Talia's direction before stopping to watch her warily. Still no motion from the woman. The mare leaned in and sampled Talia's scent. Different. Not like the men, soft, unimposing. She took a few more steps toward the female. Finally, the mare couldn't resist. She walked the rest of the way up to Talia and stood in front of her.

"Hi, pretty," Talia whispered, still not moving. The horse snorted, put her velvet muzzle against Talia's neck and sniffed loudly, nibbling her hair with her lips. Talia giggled as soft bristles tickled her neck. The mare dropped her forehead to Talia's shoulder and almost knocked her over, using her as a scratching post.

"You might want to scratch her forehead before she knocks you flat doing it herself," Hawk chuckled from the fence where he stood, watching in fascination.

Talia reached up and scratched the perfect cream star in the middle of the mare's forehead. "She's wonderful! What's her name?" Talia asked, totally absorbed in the task of scratching to the horse's obvious delight.

"That's going to be up to you," Nickolas answered from the other side of the fence. "Hawk was just the one that broke her, her mistress needs to choose her name." Talia froze. She looked up from the horse, first to Hawk, then across to Nickolas.

"What are you saying, Nick?" The fact that she'd called him by his shortened name for the first time spoke volumes.

"She's yours, Talia. We're giving her to you. I'm giving her to you."

Talia knew she should refuse the extravagant gift, but when she looked to the mare, she simply couldn't turn her away. There was a rightness in the bond forming between them. She looked back at Nickolas, tears in her eyes, and said nothing.

Nickolas was afraid he'd screwed up somehow when he saw her tears and stricken expression. Hawk, however, understood.

"It can be overwhelming, the way they move on in and take hold of your heart," he said, indicating the mare with his chin. "It's a good match; you suit."

"I have no idea what to do with her. I've never had a horse."

"Well, she's not sharing our bed like that damn tom and that's final," Nickolas joked. They all laughed, smoothing over the difficult moment and lightening the air.

"Here," Hawk said, putting the halter over the mare's head. He fastened it on the side of the mare's face before handing the rope to Talia. "Just walk off toward the barn. She'll follow." It looked like the mare would follow its mistress to the ends of the earth, halter or no, but Talia needed to learn to appear to use bridals and halters in order not to raise eyebrows, or worse yet, questions.

When they entered the barn, Talia noticed Tank stood at a post already saddled. Nickolas and Daniel followed them in, and Hawk put the new saddle and bridle on Talia's mare. Daniel saddled his own mount and led him out.

"She'll do right by you, Talia," Hawk said, holding the mare's reins out to Talia in one large, gloved hand.

They followed Nickolas and Tank out of the barn. Nickolas dropped Tank's reins on the ground in front of him. The well trained gelding stopped, waiting patiently while Nickolas took Talia by the waist and helped her mount the little mare. He adjusted her stirrups, handed her the reins and showed her how to hold them.

"This is a beautiful saddle. Is it yours, Hawk?" Talia asked, running her fingers over the ornately worked leather.

"No, I offered to marry Nickolas if he would give it to me, but he turned me down."

Talia's eyes turned to Nickolas at Hawk's teasing.

"So it's yours," she stated, still smiling at Hawk's humor.

"No, Talia, I picked it out for you. It's yours," he answered. There was something about his tone that turned her heart over.

"It's beautiful, Nickolas. I don't know what to say. It hardly seems right. You've already given me so much, and I have nothing to give you." Nickolas said nothing. He looked into her eyes for the longest time, then turned and mounted Tank. The only thing he wanted from her was forever, but he knew now was not the time to enlighten her.

~ CHAPTER THIRTY-FOUR ~

The day was clear and crisp, as was often the way with Wyoming in the spring. Talia was sitting her saddle like a natural, and her mare was taking obvious care with her new mistress as they learned to move with each other. All in all, Nickolas was very pleased.

"You let me know if you start to get tired, Talia. I don't want to leave you bow legged your first day."

"What do you mean? You turned me down this morning in bed," she smiled, delighting him.

"Riding uses different muscles. A person has to build up to it. And I remember your offer. I don't want you so saddle sore I can't take you up on it," he grinned back at her.

Suddenly a gunshot sounded from the direction Daniel had gone when he rode off to check on the sheep. Nickolas reached into his saddle scabbard, pulled out his .3006 and chambered a round.

"Sounds like Daniel's gotten into something. Do you want to stay here?" he asked her in concern, not knowing what he was riding into. He didn't want the harsh realities of ranching to put her off.

"No, I'd rather go with you."

"You sure?"

"What aren't you telling me?"

The woman was too astute by half.

"When Dan shoots, he doesn't miss. I'm not sure what he has down, but you can bet something is."

"I promise not to faint," she said, rolling her eyes, suddenly reminding him of the little warrior in desert camo he watched taking Iraq by storm.

"No, I don't suppose you will at that," he agreed, reining his mount in the direction of Daniel's shot and nudging him into a gallop. Talia and her mare followed without hesitation. As they crossed the ridge, they could see Daniel was off of his mount leaning over something on the ground. A smaller something took off at a dead serpentine run and Daniel took after it on foot. He tackled it, but it squirted out of his grasp, leaving him face down in the dust, empty handed.

Nickolas pulled the rope off of his saddle horn, and he and Tank charged after the thing, leaving Talia on the ridge to watch in amazement.

Daniel had stood up and was dusting off his Wranglers with his cowboy hat when he looked up and saw Nickolas barreling down on the bum lamb. Talia was coming off the ridge, riding towards them at a slower pace. Nickolas slid the rope over the hapless lamb's head on his way by, and wrapped a length of rope around the saddle horn. He jumped off of Tank who stopped, setting back on his hind legs, holding the rope taut while Nickolas approached the terrified lamb on the other end. Talia came up to him on her mare just as Nickolas approached the trembling, blatting lamb, running a gentle, gloved hand along its side to calm it. Reaching down, he picked it up with one arm under each set of legs while it continued to blatt piteously. He walked over to Talia and draped the lamb over her thighs, one set of its legs hanging off either side of her saddle.

Steadying the lamb across Talia's lap with one huge hand, he removed the rope from its slender neck with the other. She couldn't see his face under his cowboy hat as she looked down at him from her mount, but the contrast between the efficient roping and the gentleness in the big man as he handled the terrified lamb moved her deeply.

"Where do you think you're going with my lamb chop dinner?" Daniel teased as he approached the couple. "I saw him first!"

Talia looked at him in horror and caressed the lamb in her lap protectively. The lamb immediately calmed and quit crying at her touch.

"What happened to the mom?" Nickolas asked, indicating the bloated sheep in the distance.

"Looks like someone shot her," Daniel responded, immediately sobering as a look passed between the two men.

"That the shot we heard?" Nickolas asked.

"Nah, there were some coyotes sniffing around trying to get to the lamb. I ran them off."

"You missed?" Nickolas asked in disbelief.

"No," Daniel said, looking to Talia meaningfully and back at his brother.

"Oh," Nickolas responded, chagrined.

"Oh for heaven's sake, I shoot and kill Taliban, if you two will recall. I am not going to lose it over an old, mangy, lamb-munching coyote," Talia informed them in exasperation.

"I like her style, you going to keep her?" Daniel asked his brother.

"Hope to," Nickolas responded.

"Well, if you change your mind – "

"I won't," Nickolas said firmly.

"Figures, just my luck. I'm going to look over the ridge and see if we have any more down," Daniel informed them as he remounted his horse.

"We'll swing over to the north pasture and do the same on our way back to the ranch," Nickolas declared.

"Just drop that lamb off at the cook house, remind Loretta I like mine medium rare," Daniel threw over his shoulder. Talia snarled and sank her fingers deeper into the lamb's soft wool.

"I'll send Hawk out when we get there. Probably best to work in pairs till we get this figured out," Nickolas told his brother.

"You think I've lost my edge and can't handle myself around a couple of rustlers, bro? I'm still a Seal."

"No, you haven't lost your edge. I have. You took thirty years off my life almost getting yourself killed over there," Nickolas answered his brother. "What are *you* looking at?" he challenged Talia, "You're responsible for at least another thirty. Crap, between the two of you, I'm almost geriatric status," he complained as he remounted Tank, holding his back with a theatrical moan.

Talia was well aware of how Nickolas had just taken care to preserve his brother's pride, losing yet another little piece of her heart.

~

"I am *not* giving this lamb to Loretta," Talia informed Nickolas when he reined up in front of the cook house. He dismounted, came over and reached to take the lamb out of her lap.

"It's not sleeping with us. That's where I put my foot down," he responded with a twinkle in his eye.

"You can't really mean to have her feed this poor little thing to Daniel!"

"No, but I do mean to have her feed it."

"To who?" she demanded, voice rising in concern as she backed her mare away protectively.

"Been a tough spring," Loretta called from the porch as she came out of the cook house, putting a giant nipple on a large bottle of milk. "That's the fifth one this week. Put the poor little bugger in the shed with the rest and I'll tend to him."

"Oh, you – you – GRR!" She bared her teeth at Nickolas as he smiled up at her, the devil in his sparkling blue eyes as he took the warm lamb from her lap. "You won't get away with that one, you big jerk," she called at his retreating back as he carried the lamb to the shed for Loretta. "I know where you sleep."

~ CHAPTER THIRTY-FIVE ~

"We need to talk," Daniel addressed Nickolas as he and Hawk entered the ranch house late that afternoon. Both men looked from Nickolas to Talia meaningfully.

"She can hear anything you have to tell me," Nickolas surprised Talia by stating.

"Jimmy's dead. Shot."

Nickolas came to his feet. "How long ago?" he demanded.

"Probably last night. He was on night shift with the sheep in the high pasture. They got his big sheep dog, too. Both bodies are cold, and rig has started to set," Daniel informed him. "We left them as we found them. Didn't want to disturb any evidence, but if I were to guess, it's the same caliber we've been finding in the sheep that have been shot."

"Radio the sheriff's office. Get him and a coroner out here STAT. Offer to fly them. Hawk can pick them up in KC at the dirt strip. Where are the rest of the hands?"

"Wow is rounding them up. I've told Loretta to stay inside and away from windows. They should all be at the cook house in fifteen or so for debriefing."

"You don't debrief ranch hands. You just arm them and then set them loose to guard stock," Hawk said, reminding Daniel he wasn't commanding a bunch of trained Seals but had solid backing all the same.

"You're right, Hawk, this is really your department as far as securing the ranch is concerned. I'm better on a military operation," Daniel honored the big foreman by deferring to him.

"Not my point, just reminding you to speak their language, coz."

"I agree with Daniel," Nickolas interjected. "Hawk, you're in charge of setting up the hands to defend the ranch. I'll fly to pick up the sheriff. Daniel, you're in charge of weapons and strategy. Talia, I'll need you to protect Loretta and the cook house, so the men are freed up to work farther afield." He walked to the sizeable gun cabinet in the living room and pulled out his mother's Lady Smith & Weston. "I know you're dead accurate with a .9mm. You familiar with a revolver?"

"I prefer an auto, but I'm sure I can manage," she responded, taking the offered weapon, opening the cylinder, checking the load and closing it with expertise. Nickolas handed her a box of .357 rounds, pulled out a .280 Remington and another box of ammo.

"Has iron sights, shoots like an M-16 without the pistol grip, but only one round at a time," he instructed. "You have to cock it between rounds, like so," he said, demonstrating. "The safety is here." He handed the rifle to her along with the ammo. She ran through the process he had just shown her, familiarizing herself with the weapon. She slung the rifle over her shoulder by the strap. Nickolas handed her a leather holster for the hand gun. She slid it onto her belt and put the revolver into it.

"She's a warrior woman?" Hawk asked from where the big Indian was leaning against the door jamb, watching them.

"Yes," Nickolas and Daniel answered in unison. Hawk nodded his acceptance, no questions asked.

"You've got the cook house, then. Stay to the trees on your way down there," Hawk cautioned Talia. She nodded and slipped out the door. "Daniel, drive Nickolas to the landing strip, then meet us at the cook house. I'll radio the sheriff, finish rounding up the men and have them ready."

"Or not," Daniel stated in a resigned tone as the lights went out, casting the house in shadow. "I'll get the battery pack for the radio," he said, moving toward the office just as a rally of bullets crashed through the living room window.

Shit!

Talia was out there alone on her way to the cook house! was the first thing that went through Nickolas' mind as all three men hit the deck. Still closest to the gun cabinet, he grabbed weapons and threw them to Hawk and Daniel, sliding boxes of ammo to them across the wood floor.

WTF? Daniel mouthed to him as another round of fully auto gunfire pelleted the ranch house.

~ CHAPTER THIRTY-SIX ~

Talia heard the gunfire and knew the ranch house was under attack. She was also relatively sure it wasn't rustlers. Someone may be trying to make it appear there were rustlers on the ranch, but the style was way too organized and the gunfire clearly fully automatic, probably M-16. She would just about bet the plan was divide and conquer. Let them think the livestock was the target, get the hands all out protecting them, then strike the main ranch while it was short staffed. Crouching close to the ground in the creek bed, she continued to the cook house. There were three highly trained, intelligent, well-armed men in the ranch house. She had to trust they could hold their own for at least a little while.

The ranch hands were armed and about to burst out of the cook house when Talia rolled through the front door, coming up in a crouch at full draw. "Whoa, little lady!" Shorty exclaimed, throwing his arms in the air when he found himself looking down the barrel of the .357.

"Everyone down and get to the back room. Stay away from the windows," she ordered.

"There's shooting going on up at the big house. We need to go help," Shorty protested.

"Run out there halfcocked and you'll all be mowed down before you manage to get off the lawn," she responded. "They're packing fully automatic M-16s and god knows what else." Then, pausing and listening, "Make that M-16s and a helicopter. What do we have for fire power?"

"We all have side arms and rifles, ma'am," Shorty replied, recognizing the authority of the boss's woman.

"Any explosives?"

"There's some dynamite in the Quonset we use to blast the road open after rock slides," Alex answered.

"Can you get down there, get it and get back up here unseen?"

"Yes, ma'am."

"Great, go! But don't let that bird catch sight of you from the air. Stay covered. Who has the best eyes?"

"That would be Wow," Shorty answered. "Can't see shit – pardon me, ma'am – up close, but at distances – nothing gets past him."

"Wow, you're lookout. Take up post at the front window, but don't be seen."

"Yes, ma'am."

"Any of you a good sniper?"

"Mex, here, can pick off a coyote on the run at six hundred yards with iron sights," Shorty proudly informed her.

"See he has his choice of guns and plenty of ammo. How are you at climbing trees, Mex?"

"Well, it's been a while, ma'am, but I can still manage," the old Hispanic cowboy offered.

"Is there a can of gas by the generator out back?"

"I think so, ma'am," Whiskey said.

"Get it and bring it here, but stay low."

"Yes, ma'am."

"Loretta, how many of those milk bottles you have on hand?"

"A couple dozen."

"Bring eight clean, dry ones and a bunch of rags."

"I'm on it."

"Who's got a good pitching arm?"

"That would be Pops," someone answered.

"Two black Hummers just pulled in the main gate," Wow announced from his station, peeking through the front curtains. "The chopper has landed up next to the big house, and the Hummers look to be headed there, too."

~ CHAPTER THIRTY-SEVEN ~

From his prone position on the hardwood floor, Hawk informed Nickolas in his lazy Lakota drawl, "These ain't your garden variety rustlers."

"More like the Hole in the Wall gang on steroids," Nickolas frowned. "What can you see from over there, Daniel?"

"We've got a couple Hummers heading our way, and unless I'm mistaken, I hear a chopper. Doesn't look like any branch of the military, though, and that chopper sounds more like some civilian model, I would have to guess, some well-armed private faction." His words were drowned out in another volley as bullets tore up the wallpaper on the wall opposite the front window.

"M-16s for sure, though," Daniel calmly added when the shooting stopped. "One of us must have pissed someone off royal."

"Can you see Talia?" Nickolas asked in concern.

"No, but I wouldn't expect to. She's a pro, Nickolas. We're out gunned and pinned down. She's in a much better position than we are."

A deep voice with a Spanish accent yelled from the enemy camp, "You're boxed in. All we want is the Martin woman. Send her out and we'll leave."

"Well, now at least we know who it was that pissed someone off," Daniel stated. "The good news is, they think she's still in here. Care to respond?" he asked his brother.

"Nah, I'm not even going to honor that with an insult. Just how dumb do they take us for?" His words were no sooner out of his mouth when another rally struck the front of the house.

"Throw out some cover fire. I'm headed to the back shed," Hawk ordered from the back of the house.

"Okay, we've got your six," Daniel called back, pulling out two revolvers and dashing across the room while firing through the window. As soon as he was out of ammo and down to reload, Nickolas followed suit from the other direction.

"What's he up to?" Daniel wanted to know.

"Fuck if I know what's in that damned Indian's brain, but you can bet it bodes ill for the dickheads out there."

Several minutes and numerous volleys of fire later, Hawk reappeared through the back door, dragging a short Hispanic man in by the nape. The man sported numerous contusions, a black eye and was barely conscious. Hawk had three bandoleros slung over one shoulder and two assault rifles over the other.

"Nice coup, coz!" Daniel crowed as Hawk threw him one of the rifles. "Nope, not military. This puppy is black market style. It's actually an AR-15 with the serial numbers filed off, and it's been converted to fully auto after market."

"What's with the slime bag?" Nickolas asked, indicating the captive as Hawk threw his cousin the other rifle and he caught it midair.

"Thought I could use some of my ancestor's techniques and twist some intel out of the little bastard," Hawk replied with an evil gleam in his eye.

"Good thinking! Don't you want to keep this, though? You scored it," Nickolas asked his cousin, indicating the assault rifle.

"Nah, you're better with it than I am," Hawk replied, reloading his .3006 and checking his hand guns. Reaching into the gun cabinet, he pulled out his uncle's old bull whip, pulled the knife out of its scabbard at his hip and cut off several lengths of leather. He proceeded to hogtie the hapless captive with them. "Wakey wakey, dickhead, I didn't hit you that hard," Hawk taunted the semiconscious man, waving his hunting knife under his nose. "It's about docking time at the ol' corral, and I could use some practice. Want to volunteer your worthless balls?" The man came to full wakefulness, terror in his eyes.

"The chopper has set down on the rise, and they're coming in closer with the Hummers," Daniel reported from the front room. "Fuck, there's a machine gun mounted on top of one of 'em! What next? A frigging rocket launcher?" The front room window took another battering and finally gave up the fight, the remaining glass imploding into the house, and the frame sagging dangerously. "It's not looking good for the home team, boys."

Suddenly, the gunner manning the machine gun slumped over the hood, and the big gun silenced. After a short span, the retort of a .3006 could be heard. Another man climbed up to replace the gunner, but didn't get a single shot off before he, too, fell, and another delayed retort echoed off the red cliffs.

"Shit! We have backup!" Daniel reported.

"Open fire, and take out as many of the bastards as we can before they manage to rally," Nickolas ordered.

"Roger that, bro."

They had not managed to empty a full clip when a huge explosion rent the air. "WTF?" Nickolas wanted to know.

"Looks like the chopper was just blown into the next county!" Daniel reported from his post at the side of the ruined window. Looking the other direction, he exclaimed, "Lay down fire, we have a ranch truck coming our way! Shit! Pops is standing up in the bed getting ready to throw something. Cover him!"

Another massive explosion followed as one of the Hummers went airborne. Men poured out of the wreckage the minute it hit ground, clothes on fire, running and screaming only to be dropped by Nickolas' AR-15.

"They're taking another pass. Oh, Jesus Christ, Talia's at the wheel!" Daniel reported just before another explosion rent the air.

Nickolas died a thousand deaths. Standing, he dashed for the front door, AR-15 blazing as he ran to cover his woman. In slow motion, he saw the Hispanic man drop to one knee, aiming at the cab of the truck. Pops stood again, lit another molotov cocktail and hurled it at the remaining Hummer. Nickolas mowed the assailant down, but not before the man got off a shot at the truck. The ranch truck swerved and came up on two wheels. Pops dropped back down into the bed. The truck righted itself just before coming to a stop as the last Hummer blew sky high. Nickolas headed toward the ranch truck at a dead run while Daniel took care of the collateral damage, mowing down anything that moved from the enemy quadrant.

Nickolas tore the driver's side door open and came face to face with the business end of a .357.

"Oh geez, Nick, you could give a girl some warning!" Talia exclaimed, aiming the Lady S&W skyward upon recognizing him. The windshield of the truck was blown out and there was glass all over his woman, who lay prone on her back across the bench seat of the old ranch truck. Several small cuts peppered her beautiful face. Her hair had come loose from its tie and flowed around her in a silken fall. Her eyes were shining with adrenalin and something else he didn't want to examine too closely, not yet.

"This is not acceptable," he stated as he grabbed her by the front of her shirt and dragged her out of the truck. Standing her up, he dusted off the glass shards, and examined every inch of her, looking for damage. "You're supposed to be safe here. I'm supposed to keep you safe!" he whispered as he pulled her into his arms and placed his forehead against hers. She was steady, rock solid. He was shaking like a leaf.

~ CHAPTER THIRTY-EIGHT ~

The screams that rent the air were agonizing to hear. "What the heck is that?" Talia wanted to know.

"I think Hawk has a tomahawk to grind with the one survivor," Nickolas informed her.

"What's he doing?"

"Gathering intel," Daniel informed her as he sauntered into the cook house, cowboy heels clicking on the linoleum floor. "Hey, Loretta, is there any whisky to be had? For medicinal purposes, of course. My nerves are shot, and it beats Prozac," he added, tongue in cheek.

Loretta appeared, a tray of glasses on one arm and a bottle of Jim Beam in the other hand. "Liquid Prozac all 'round," she announced, placing both on the cook house table with a resounding clatter. "For medicinal purposes only, you understand."

Another scream sounded from the big house on the hill.

"Nickolas? What is Hawk doing to him?" Talia asked in concern.

"If I know our coz? Torturing him with the idea of all the things he could do to torture him."

"In other words, shaving his balls in preparation for docking," Daniel helpfully filled in.

"What is docking?" Talia wanted to know.

"Removing the male parts of a ram," Loretta happily supplied.

"Oh!"

"Here, baby, have some liquid Prozac," Nickolas said, offering her a glass containing a good two fingers of the amber liquid.

"Thanks, don't mind if I do."

"Did you see that chopper go up after Alex rigged the dynamite?" Shorty exclaimed.

"Did *you* see Mex drop the machine gunners?" Wow enthused.

"Yeah, but Boss's woman and Pops in the ranch truck with Loretta's molotov cocktails stole the show!" Mex said excitedly.

"Oh, god, give me strength," Nickolas groaned.

"Dare I ask who organized the coup?" asked Daniel.

"Boss's woman," they all answered in unison, admiration, devotion and awe in their tone.

"Oh, god, give me strength," Nickolas repeated, slapping a hand to his forehead.

~

Hawk's somewhat unorthodox methods were rewarded by intel as to where the assault on the ranch had originated. Apparently, there was a very rich man somewhere in Colombia that had developed an interest in Talia's "gifts" and had paid big to obtain her. Hawk was unable to find out anything further. The captive was more afraid of his boss than of the formidable

Indian with a knife in his hand. The hapless captive had been turned over to authorities, but a sniper had put a bullet through the rear window of the sheriff's SUV and into the back of the informant's head on the way into town. The assassination left Talia with no doubt the threat to the ranch still remained.

~ CHAPTER THIRTY-NINE ~

Leaving was going to be the hardest thing she'd ever done, Talia thought as she packed her bag and secured her cats in their carriers. When she informed Nickolas of her decision, all color left his face, and he recoiled as if she'd struck him. Just the memory of it broke her heart. But, how could she stay, knowing she endangered the entire ranch?

He'd stood there silently, devastation clearly written all over his handsome, raw boned face - then nodded once and left the room. She had not seen him since. God, how was she going to live without him?

"You ready?" Hawk asked from the bedroom door. He'd agreed to take her to town in the Cessna.

"Yes." She looked around the bedroom where she had shared so much with the man she loved beyond all reason.

Hawk drove her to the landing strip in the Rover, pulled the Cessna out of the hanger and loaded her luggage and the cat carriers. He completed his preflight and opened the passenger side door. Talia got in, fastening her seatbelt. Her eyes kept searching the area, hoping for a glimpse of Nickolas, but he was nowhere to be seen.

The tears hit after takeoff as they cleared the red cliffs and banked west toward the setting sun. She looked out the passenger window at the ranch she'd come to love, letting the tears silently wash down her cheeks unchecked.

After a time, Hawk spoke. "I'm not much with words, but I need to say my piece. I have $300,000.00 cash here in my pocket." He patted the front of his denim jacket. "Nickolas gave it to me for you to use on a new start. I will give it to you, take you to the airport in Casper and put you on a commercial flight to wherever you want to go if you can just assure me of one thing. Tell me that you don't love Nickolas."

Talia looked into the big Indian's face in shock, searching his eyes. She looked to her hands where they were folded in her lap, saying nothing.

"My cousin is a natural born hero. He has been protecting people all his life, including me when I was too small to do it myself. In all the years I have known him, he has never demanded anything for himself and has received nothing but hard knocks for all his efforts. You leavin'? Well, it is just likely to be the one hard knock he won't recover from. He won't impose himself on you, but he'll follow and protect you from a distance until they take him out. Or – you can stay here with family where you both have a fightin' chance." Hawk suddenly banked the Cessna and dropped low over the flat top of a bluff. Without warning, he sat the craft down.

"What are you doing?" Talia asked the big man in alarm.

"I'm givin' you a chance to rethink your position before you make the biggest mistake of both your lives, ma'am. Down there?" he indicated an old log home nearly concealed by the huge red bluff they'd landed on. "That's the original homestead. We keep it stocked, but no roads access it anymore." He shut down the Cessna's engine, got out and unloaded one of Talia's bags. Setting it on the ground, he circled the craft and opened the passenger door. "Unless you want me to touch you, you might want to get out under your own steam," he threatened, causing Talia to scramble out of the plane. Hawk closed the door, walked back around the plane and got back in.

"Clear!" he yelled out the small side window, firing up the engine. Talia wisely stepped back. Hawk taxied the Cessna to the other end of the bluff and turned around. The engine roared as he took off, catching air just as the craft fell off the end of the cliff and banked back toward the way they had come.

Talia stood in the fading light and the silence left in the wake of the Cessna's engine. The big bastard had just dumped her off in BF who-knows-where and flew off into the sunset with her cats, she realized in utter disbelief.

~

Nickolas almost fell off of Tank when he saw the Cessna headed back to the ranch. Hawk gave him a wing wag as he passed overhead, indicating Talia was at the old homestead rather than on a flight out of his life. Nickolas was weak with relief. There was still a chance.

Earlier that day, Hawk had found Nickolas in the barn gathering up leather straps after Talia had informed him she was leaving.

"What those for, coz?" he had asked, indicating the leather ties.

"I am going to fucking well tie her to my fucking bed!" Nickolas had responded.

"TMI!"

"She's going to leave me, Hawk," Nickolas had said in agony. Hawk looked as stricken as Nickolas felt.

"I don't think tying her to your bed is your best course of action."

"She hasn't given me enough time," Nickolas agonized. "I need more time to make her love me."

257

"Don't think the leather is going to do it. She doesn't strike me as the type," Hawk had advised. He'd sat down with Nickolas and outlined a plan, one where Hawk was the bad guy and Nickolas possibly got more time. Both men eventually agreed that if Talia truly didn't want to be with Nickolas that he had to let her go.

Nickolas had gone to the safe and put together a large amount of his personal funds for Hawk to give her if it became clear she truly didn't want him. He wanted her to have another house, and he would damn well see she was provided for the rest of her life. He would protect her at any cost, but he would let her go. He loved her enough to let her go.

Now, here he was on his way to the original homestead where Hawk had left her. They would be alone, and he would, by god, win her love no matter how long it took. He coaxed Tank into an easy gallop, eating up the miles as he rode into the magnificent sunset fire of Wyoming.

~ CHAPTER FORTY ~

Talia had run out of creative names to call Hawk by the time she managed to struggle down the side of the bluff and make her way to the log cabin with her bag. She dragged the carry-on sized luggage the final distance and up onto the wraparound porch just as the birds set into their evening chorus. The sky lit up in a pink, red and orange display that took her breath away in spite of her ire. God, how she loved this country, this ranch and the man who ran it, she thought as she sat down on the porch step, put her elbows on her knees and her chin in her hands to watch the sunset.

When the sky finally faded to indigo and the evening star appeared, she started to chill. She stood and entered the darkening interior of the cabin, found a lantern and some matches, and lit it. The cabin was surprisingly large for its vintage. It boasted a large country kitchen with a well-stocked walk-in pantry, a dining room, separate living room, a wash room off of the kitchen and three bedrooms. No indoor plumbing or running water, she noted, but there was an outhouse out back that she had passed on her way down the hill, and an old well with a hand pump in a small gazebo out front. There was a fireplace in the living room, a wood burning cook stove in the kitchen and large wood burning stove in the open sitting area next to the bedrooms. The sitting area sported two platform rockers separated by an old, scarred end table with a brass lantern on it, and three floor-to-ceiling built in book shelves, full of leather bound books. There was plank flooring throughout, and Pendleton blankets covered the beds. With the exception of a little dust, the place was spotless and well kept.

Talia lit the lantern in the sitting room and opened the stove. Split wood and kindling was stacked neatly in a wood box next to it. A pile of old newspapers in a round barrel next to the box had a box of farmer's matches on top. She wadded up some newspaper and put it into the stove, added some kindling, and topped it all off with some of the smaller pieces of split wood. Striking a match, she set it to blaze, only to have smoke start rolling into the room at an alarming rate.

Dusty, size twelve cowboy boots appeared in her line of sight, and one long arm reached past her to the stovepipe to turn a lever. Talia screamed and nearly jumped out of her skin. Standing up suddenly, she found herself surrounded by the huge, rock solid mass that was Nickolas' chest, as his big denim clad arms came around to steady her.

"Damper," his deep voice rumbled in her ear as he nuzzled her neck from behind.

"What?" she breathed.

"Damper, you have to open the damper, or all the smoke comes into the house."

"Oh." She was still shaking, whether from shock or his nearness, she couldn't say.

Abruptly, he lifted her into his arms and carried her into the largest of the three bedrooms, depositing her on the bed.

"You have exactly one minute to lose the clothes before I start cutting them off of you," he informed her, throwing his cowboy hat onto the chair. He loomed over her from his six foot five height, removing his knife from its scabbard on his leather belt. Talia sat up and tried to scramble off the bed in indignation, but he pressed his huge hand into the center of her chest, grabbing her blouse and slitting it down the front with the sharp knife. He removed her bra in the same efficient manner and proceeded to shred her jeans from her body. Talia was frozen in shock. While he could be rough in his passion, he had never been unkind. She looked up into his face to find a tight lipped, icy, iron resolve as he cut off her panties and pulled off her boots and socks, leaving her naked among the remnants of her ruined clothing on the bed.

She tried again to sit up, but he pressed his big, warm, callused palm directly between her full breasts and pinned her to the mattress on her back. Reaching behind him, he drew leather ties from the hip pocket of his Wranglers. He pulled one of her arms over her head and pinned it with his knee, then tied a soft leather strap around her wrist and to the bed post. After repeating the action with the other wrist, he tied her ankles to the posts at the foot of the bed while she struggled to no avail. Cowboy that he was, he was fast and efficient with his knots, his superior size giving him every advantage. She had absolutely no chance at all against him. He stood and looked down on her in silence, his expression unreadable, then turned and left the room.

When he returned some minutes later, he had removed his denim jacket. The sleeves of his flannel shirt were rolled up, and he carried a steaming bowl of water, a cup, a leather kit and a razor strop. A hand towel was thrown over one large forearm. Her eyes widened in fear at the sight of the leather strop in his big hand. He looked into her face, some emotion flickering behind his ice blue eyes. He shook his head in silence, turned his back to her, and placed all of the articles on the antique lavatory next to the bed.

Nickolas didn't miss the fear in her beautiful gray eyes. She thought he would actually take a strop to her velvet skin? God, that hurt. She must not know him at all, but she would, *she by god would* before they left the cabin. She would know him, soul deep. This, he swore.

There was nothing he could say to her. He had said it all the last time she tried to leave him. This time, he would have to show her the only way left to him. He buckled the strop to the towel bar on the lavatory, and pulled his straight razor out of the leather shaving kit.

As Nickolas started sharpening the straight razor on the leather strop, Talia began shaking in earnest, terror filling her eyes as she watched him from the bed.

"Nickolas, please let me go," she pleaded. He looked down at her and silently shook his head, never missing a stroke of the blade over leather. He tested it on the hair of his forearm. Seemingly satisfied, he set the razor on the lavatory.

He dipped the towel in the bowl of water and rung it out. Folding it expertly, he approached her and gently placed it over her mound. It was hot, too hot, almost painfully so on her unprotected flesh. Nickolas picked up the cup and pulled a shaving brush out of the kit. Dipping the brush in the bowl of water, he rubbed it in the cup, building a thick lather before picking the razor up and approaching her.

He sat on the bed next to her, crossed his legs, rested his forearms on his knee with the razor in one hand and the cup and brush in the other. He looked at her with laser blue eyes and an unreadable expression.

God, but she was beautiful like this, bound spread-eagle on his bed. He hated the fear in her eyes when she looked at him, at the same time wanting her with every fiber of his being. He set the cup on the bed and removed the towel from her pretty mound. Lifting the brush, he lathered her pubic area with gentle, provocative strokes, taking care to brush her tight little nub on every pass. She took in a breath and squirmed, eyes darkening. Nickolas took the straight razor and shaved her pubis with precise strokes, taking every care not to nick her delicate flesh.

Talia wisely held still during the procedure, but her eyes were almost black and her breathing harsh as she watched him in trepidation. When he had carefully wiped the last of the lather from her, he sat back and looked down at his handiwork.

Her pretty pussy was flushed and bare. He almost came in his Wranglers before he savagely clamped down on his lust. Reaching out, he ran his thick, callused forefinger down her cleft and pressed it inside, finding her wet and hot for him. He pulled his finger back out, and put it into his mouth as he looked into her eyes.

Talia almost came undone at his first touch and the sight of him sampling her cream. God, but the man was a study in carnal virile sexuality! She could feel her freshly shaved sex dripping for want of him.

Nickolas stood and removed the shaving equipment from the room. Talia could hear him stoking the fire just before he returned to the lantern lit bedroom. He had a shoe box in his hand that he placed on the lavatory, going through the contents with his back turned to her.

When he turned around, he had a feather in his hand. He sat on the bed, still fully dressed, and ran the large, soft feather over one nipple, then the next. Talia moaned, arching off the bed. After tormenting her taught nipples until she was sure she would explode, he ran the feather down the middle of her chest to her navel and across her mound, caressing her nub with short, gentle strokes. She fought her bonds, legs trembling as her head thrashed back and forth.

Setting the feather aside, he climbed onto the bed between her spread legs, and pressed her knees further apart to deliver an open mouthed kiss to her core. Talia cried out and he lifted his head, looking into her eyes. His eyes were flashing blue flame as he turned his head and bit the tendon where her leg met her

263

mound. He licked away the sting and bit the other side. Returning to her clitoris, he laved it lazily and gripped it between his front teeth with an almost painful bite, lashing it with his tongue. She writhed beneath him, moaning his name.

Continuing to pay undivided attention to her swollen little nub, he sank one long finger into her wet slit, and she arched into his mouth. He removed his finger, and she whimpered in protest until he drove back into her wet depths with two fingers. She shook uncontrollably while he stroked in and out with long deep thrusts, rotating his wrist. She was right there on the edge, about to tumble over when he suddenly stopped and pulled away from her.

He got off the bed and looked down at her flushed, wet core, his eyes traveling up to her taught berry-red nipples and passion filled eyes, while he slowly unsnapped his shirt. He let it slide off of his massive shoulders, exposing his muscular chest.

Talia longed to run her hands over his tanned flesh as it glistened in the soft lamplight. He toed off his cowboy boots, removed his sox and stood up, unfastening his heavy silver belt buckle and unbuttoning his Wranglers. When he shucked his jeans, his swollen member sprang free, leaving her no doubt that he wanted her, but he made no move to take her. Instead he stood over her, slowly stroking himself and looking down at her swollen, wet mound. God, she wanted that inside her right now! Hope rose in her chest when he climbed onto the bed, but he settled his face between her legs instead. Sinking his tongue into her saturated depths, he licked her slit and nibbled at her clitoris, repeating the routine until she was on the edge of exploding.

Suddenly he stood up and away from the bed, eyes blazing down at her, rampant member straining away from his body. She could see it throb with his every heartbeat, and from the dance it was doing, his heart was just about to beat itself out of his chest. He palmed the tortured member and stroked himself while looking down into her eyes. Faster, harder, he fisted himself until his eyes glazed over and he cried out her name, his eyes never leaving hers as his cum shot into his hand and across her breasts.

Nickolas took the towel, cleaned off his hands then her breasts. Leaning over, he held the full mounds together and suckled both nipples at once until she writhed in desire. He nipped one hard bud, then the other, until she was sure they were raw, before suckling them again. She could feel it clear to her womb. Could a woman come from a man's suckling? she wondered, just before he quit.

He worked his way down her body with open mouthed kisses until he settled between her legs. He suckled her clitoris and sank three fingers into her with a brutal rotating thrust, driving in and out until she was about to go up in smoke. She could feel her orgasm building and nearly rolling over her, when he pulled off of her once more as he stood up, fully aroused and throbbing. He fisted himself again and started to stroke. This time his knees almost buckled as he savagely pounded himself until he roared his release, holding her eyes with his.

He cleaned up and returned to the writhing, whimpering woman on the bed, and devoured her bare, enflamed core while she screamed for the release he denied her. Just as she was about to crest, he lifted his head and looked into her face from between her legs. Tears ran unchecked down her flushed face, her lower lip swollen from where she had repeatedly bit it in her passion. Her hair was a wild, tangled mess from her struggles, her wild eyes pleaded into his, and his heart broke.

"Please, Nickolas," she whimpered.

"Please what, baby?" he finally spoke, his voice raspy with passion.

"Please, I want you," she begged.

"You left me," he reminded her. "Now you want me?"

"I've always wanted you," she sobbed.

"If I take you again, I will never let you go. I'm going to fuck you until you love me, Talia, until you can't bear the thought of being without me inside you. I'm going to make you want me like I want you, love me like I love you. If it takes the rest of my life keeping you in this bed on the edge of heaven, I am going to, *by god*, make you mine."

"Nickolas, please don't hurt me anymore, I hurt to have you inside me. Please."

Nickolas froze, looking down at the ravaged bound woman in his bed. "I never wanted to hurt you, baby, I just want your love," he whispered as his magnificent laser blue eyes suddenly filled with tears.

"Oh, Nickolas, you already have it. It's been yours from the first time you took me. My body and my heart are a package deal."

"I want to plant my children here," he said, laying his big palm over her belly. "I want to watch them suckle here," he whispered as he reverently caressed her breast. "I want my ring on your finger, for you to take my name for your own, Talia. I want forever, baby, I can't let you go."

"Okay."

"Okay what?" Nickolas asked, confused.

"Okay to all that, now will you please fuck me before I die from wanting you?"

"Not like this, baby, I can't drive myself into your bound body."

"Why not?"

"I am too wild for wanting you. I could hurt you," His voice was hoarse with passion as he pulled the knife from his belt on the floor, and cut her bonds.

After rubbing the red marks on her ankles and wrists in apology, he lay on his back, his glorious engorged member reaching well above his navel. He put his hands above his head and grasped the headboard, meeting her eyes. "Take me as you will, do whatever you like. Wreak your revenge, baby, just never leave me."

Talia didn't need any further encouragement. She leaned over him, her long, soft hair pooling on his belly, and took him into her mouth. Nickolas almost broke the solid oak headboard as he arched off the bed. She licked and suckled him, cradling his taught sack in one hand until he shook from head to toe, his pelvis thrusting convulsively. She lifted her head, and looked him in the eye while she continued to stroke her soft hands up and down his thick shaft.

"This, and every drop of seed that comes out of it, is mine," she announced. "You want to get off? I expect to be involved."

"Yes, ma'am."

Talia prowled up his body like a cat, straddled his hips and pressed the engorged head of his member into the entrance of her hot core. She braced her tiny hands on his broad chest, sinking down until she took her fill. She paused. He could feel her fist tight muscles spasming around him, adjusting to his size. She looked into his eyes and started to move with agonizingly slow thrusts.

"I love it when you lose it with me and drive in so far I can't tell where I end and you begin. I love it when you hold me so tight

267

you leave marks and I feel your hot seed filling me. I love how you love me, Nickolas," she said. Her eyes never leaving his, she increased her pace until she was wild, lifting high and grinding deep until they both exploded.

"And Nickolas?"

"Yes, baby?" he gasped.

"I love you."

"Are you sure? I want you to be sure," he said with a wicked grin as he rolled her over, pulled her legs up to his hips, and sank into her willing body again.

~ CHAPTER FORTY-ONE ~

"I can't move, don't make me move, Nickolas," Talia whimpered piteously as he entered their bedroom fully dressed, a bowl of steaming water in his hands. He sat the bowl on the lavatory and pulled out a washcloth. After he wrung it out, he soaped it up with a fragrant bar from the china dish on the lavatory.

"This will help. Let me tend you, baby," he offered, as he pressed the warm cloth between her legs and gently bathed her.

They had made wild love all night until neither could move, sleeping in each other's arms, sated. He felt badly he'd not been more careful with her. She was, after all, mostly inexperienced, and much smaller than he was. He had ravaged her repeatedly. Never mind she had encouraged him every step of the way, demanding every burning thrust. He was the experienced one. It was his responsibility to take care of his woman.

"Nothing is going to help. I'm never going to walk again."

"Oh, yes you will. I have plans."

"No! Don't touch me!"

"Not those kind of plans, at least not until you heal. Other plans."

"Tell me, so I can tell you to fuck off."

"No, now Talia, we agreed, remember? No getting off without you."

She groaned.

"First, I'll make you breakfast and serve you in bed if you like," he began.

"No, not in bed, that's scene of the crime."

"Okay, not the bed – at the dining room table. I'll put a soft pillow in your chair."

Another groan.

"Then we'll get you dressed, and go sit on the porch on the swing. I'll bring the pillow."

~

Nickolas had been right. Talia felt immeasurably better after being bathed and treated with a tin of healing salve. Belly full, she sat on the promised soft pillow next to Nickolas on the porch swing, sipping coffee and watching the sun break over the red cliffs.

"It's so beautiful here, Nickolas," she breathed in awe.

"Do you like the ranch, Talia?"

"Oh yes, I love it."

"We don't have to stay here if you think you'll feel isolated. I'll live with you wherever you want, baby."

"But you need to run the ranch," she said, surprised.

"The ranch can go to hell. It's not worth losing you."

"I love it here. I don't feel isolated, more like I'm finally where I belong," she assured him, struggling to describe her feelings for the land.

"We can remodel the big house any way you like, or for that matter, build you a new one somewhere else on the property if that one holds bad memories."

"I don't need anything extravagant," she insisted, wondering where he was going with this.

He suddenly stood and dropped down on one knee in front of the swing. Reaching into his front pocket, he pulled out a velvet box and opened it, handing it to her.

"Marry me, Talia," he demanded, his heart in his eyes.

"I thought we were already married."

"Just common law. I want to have an official ceremony, for you to take my name. I want to do it right with you, Talia." He pulled the sparkling diamond ring out of the box, and, taking her left hand, he placed it on her ring finger. "If you don't like it, we can change it out for whatever you want," he offered.

"Okay."

"Okay what?"

"Okay, I'll marry you, Nickolas," she said, tears in her eyes as she looked down at the exquisite ring on her hand, and back up into the laser blue eyes of the man she loved beyond all reason.

~ CHAPTER FORTY-TWO ~

Their wedding day dawned clear and bright, not a cloud in the sky, the ever present Wyoming wind obvious by its absence. Hawk had been sent on numerous buying trips into town, but he took it in stride with his typical, silent good nature. He had been on his way to the Cessna on one of those trips last week when Talia ran after him, stopping him before he left in the Rover for the landing strip. Nickolas died a thousand deaths as he watched his woman have a very serious discussion with his cousin, trying to get him to take something, and his cousin staunchly refusing. Was she trying to leave again? he agonized. She was clearly trying to hide something from him.

"Please, Hawk, it's all I have, and I really want you to pick up the package for me," she pleaded with the big Indian.

"I'll get your package, and you can pay me back later," Hawk insisted, refusing the small box containing her pearl earrings. "I know his size, and I know the right style. You don't have to part with these or settle for whatever they will bring you in trade."

"But I have no idea when I can repay you."

"Oh, probably before you can even imagine," the big man responded mysteriously. He pulled away and drove to the strip without accepting her box, darn the obstinate man.

Talia sipped her coffee in fond memory of their encounter. He had definitely come through for her, and he'd been so right. Better to get the right one and pay him back later, than to settle for something lesser. After all, she planned on this one lasting a lifetime.

"You ready to get dressed, little girl?" Loretta loudly inquired as she approached the newly remodeled ranch house porch. She was taking her role as matron of honor like she did everything else, with gusto. "The groom is pacing a hole in the cook house linoleum, and tugging at his tie until I fear we will have to replace it with a bolo before we get you two hitched. Preacher man is here, all it lacks is one bride."

~

"You got the ring?" Nickolas asked his brother for the fifth time.

"Yup, right here in my pocket, just like the last four times you asked me," Daniel answered, patting his front pants pocket and suppressing a grin. He had never seen the big agent so nervous.

"Looks like Hawk's bringing 'em down now!" Mex alerted the men, pointing to the Rover as it headed down the dirt road between the cook house and the ranch house, leaving a trail of red dust in its wake. "Better get out there and lined up under the trees like our lady said."

The men headed out with the minister, and stood on the lawn under the big cottonwoods while the Rover pulled up on the other side of the cook house. After long, agonizing moments, a Native American flute started to play a haunting melody.

WTF? Nickolas looked at his brother.

"Damned if I know," Daniel stated, just as confused.

The cook house screen door opened and Loretta walked out, tottering on moderately high heels, wearing a lovely powder blue dress and carrying a bouquet of purple flowers. A matching sprig of violets graced her upswept gray hair.

"Would you look at that!" Shorty exclaimed in admiration, an appreciative gleam in his eyes.

"Ah sh—I mean shoot," Wow corrected himself, glancing at the preacher. "Another one bites the dust."

"I mean, I, uhh – I'm just sayin' – look at 'er!" Shorty stuttered.

Loretta joined the men, blushing prettily. The flute music shifted, and the screen door opened again. Standing on the porch was the most amazing sight Nickolas had ever seen. Decked out in a western suit and dress boots with his long black hair neatly braided down his back stood his cousin, flute in hand, playing the most haunting melody he'd ever heard. Standing next to, but carefully not touching the big Indian, was the most beautiful woman in the world. Talia scarcely reached Hawk's shoulder in her high heels. She was a vision in gossamer white, carrying a bouquet of violets, her long skirts and long loose hair lifting in the soft Wyoming breeze. In that moment Nickolas knew she was the only woman he had ever loved. They walked forward, side by side, his woman and his cousin, while his brother stood proudly at his side. The moment would be etched in his heart forever.

The ceremony went by in a blur, Nickolas so absorbed in his woman that he had to be prompted to say his vows. When the time came, Daniel dutifully handed the preacher Talia's ring, a beautiful diamond inlayed band that perfectly matched her engagement ring. Loretta surprised Nickolas by handing the preacher a large man's band she had apparently been wearing on her thumb. Vows were exchanged, rings slid on fingers. When Nickolas looked at the ring Talia had proudly slid onto his hand, he was so shaken, he almost lost his train of thought. It was the perfect replica of her wedding band, inlayed with sparkling baguette diamonds in an artful twist of yellow and white gold.

"You may kiss the bride," the preacher announced. Nickolas could do that, yes, that he could manage…

"You may stop kissing the bride any time now," the preacher's humored voice, accompanied by snickers and guffaws from the onlookers, finally penetrated Nickolas' fogged brain.

~ CHAPTER FORTY-THREE ~

"Oh Nickolas! I don't know what to say. It is just….just…." Talia gave up and burst into tears.

"Jesus, baby, it's only a frigging camera," Nickolas defended himself, totally undone by her tears. "Now I'm half afraid to take you in and show you the rest," he grouched.

"It's not just a camera! It's a digital Nikon with all the bells and whistles with a butt-load of lenses. Would you look at that telephoto!" she enthused, fondling the long lenses in question. Nickolas had visions of her fondling him instead, and had to shake his head to refocus.

"Baby, please don't cry," he begged, taking her into his arms and wiping her tears with his big thumbs. They stood on the new porch of the ranch house as a breeze kicked up, blowing the long white skirts of her wedding dress across his legs in a gossamer embrace. He leaned down and took her sweet mouth in a gentle, sensual kiss. "Come on inside so I can show you the rest."

He led her into the add-on that had been under construction and off limits for the past month. Opening the French doors, he motioned her inside. The room was large and airy with a huge bank of windows. There was a large desk built in with top-of-the-line computer equipment and a huge flat screen monitor. On one side of the room was an open closet, sporting many shelves covered with various papers and supplies, and more camera equipment, including several tripods and telephoto lenses. She looked back at him in amazement.

"We now have satellite internet. They say it's top speed and should be able to manage anything you want to do. There are both PCs and Macs so you can play well with others. Daniel arranged for the latest Photoshop programs, along with Flash and god only knows what else. Talia Pane Graphic Design is up and running," Nickolas announced, searching her eyes. "Baby? Don't cry again. Okay?"

"But I have nothing to give you, Nickolas."

"Baby, you've given me your love, my life back, my brother's life. This is nothing compared to that."

"What the hell you two still doing in here?" Daniel demanded from the door. "Hawk has the Cessna fired up. Everyone is waiting with bucket loads of rice. Let's get this show on the road."

"Where are we going?" Talia asked.

"To the old homestead to honeymoon. I thought it only fitting," Nickolas smiled down at her.

"You got my soft pillow and that tin of salve?"

"You betcha, ma'am."

ABOUT THE AUTHOR

Having been brought up overseas and living with local families in many cultures, Cahira O'Donnell has a rich history to draw upon.

Armed with her history, combined with a degree in Psychology and a deep understanding of human nature, Cahira creates multifaceted characters and stories that are engaging, dynamic, realistic and boldly erotic.

Cahira now lives in the beautiful mountains of Colorado where she enjoys kayaking, back packing with her adult children, a quiet home, beautiful scenery and immersing herself in the art of storytelling.

If you like:

Christine Freehan
Laurann Dohner
Katherine Mann
Lora Leagh
Cindy Gerard

You will love

Cahira O'Donnell

To learn more about Cahira and her novels visit:
www.cahiraodonnell.com

Read on for a look at

GHOST HAWK

Book Two of the exciting

SEVEN SISTERS SERIES

By Cahira O'Donnell

Coming Soon!

From Dark River Publishing

CAHIRA O'DONNELL

GHOST HAWK

THE SEVEN SISTERS SERIES
BOOK TWO

GHOST HAWK

Coming 2014

~ CHAPTER ONE ~

She was going to die right here, on her face, in a snow drift in the Wyoming wind. She knew it was just a matter of time, but she was out of resources. She had given it a good run. In the end, the military hadn't managed to get her, but the elements would.

The Hummer lay on its roof some miles back. It had rolled when she'd lost control and driven off an embankment of the remote dirt road. The ground blizzard had concealed the sharp turn until it was too late. She'd crashed through a barbed wire fence and down a ravine, rolling at least three times before coming to a stop upside down.

When she regained consciousness, gas was leaking into the interior of the vehicle, and the wind was howling relentlessly through the broken windows. Dazed and hurt in more places than she could count, she'd had the presence of mind to get out of the Hummer before it caught fire, to seek shelter elsewhere. A great plan, with only one drawback – there was no shelter to be found for miles – no trees, no buildings, not even a large rock to huddle behind. She encountered nothing but endless prairie, snow drifts and glacier winds that pelleted her numb face with snow.

The remote country road was not used or, for that matter, passable in the winter, so she knew there was no hope of rescue. She had trudged through the deep snow for what seemed like hours, until falling where she now lay, exhausted and numb. She could feel peace stealing over her, and knew she was freezing to death. Oh well, there were worse ways to go, and she was bone weary of running. Closing her silver, starlit eyes, she surrendered to the inevitable.

~ Chapter Two ~

The lone rider pulled his cowboy hat further down on his brow, tilting his head into the wind to protect his face. As his dependable paint struggled through snow that rose above the stirrups in the deeper drifts, Hawk leaned forward, giving the horse its head. He trusted the animal's unerring ability to find home even in the most violent blizzard. Unexpectedly, horse and rider came upon a downed section of fence. Hawk reined in his mount and examined the area. It didn't take him long to locate the upside down Hummer, half buried in snow. He was relieved to see there was no one inside, but there were faint tracks, almost erased by the blowing snow, leading away from the ruined vehicle. He knew he really needed to mend the fence before they lost livestock, but the tracks were uneven and unusually small. There was also a blood trail he discovered when he dismounted, and carefully brushed snow aside to examine the prints more closely.

Hawk was an excellent tracker, having learned from his Lakota grandfather. It was clear to him that an injured female, weighing no more than one hundred and ten pounds, had walked away from the wrecked vehicle, alone, into the unprotected prairie. There was no shelter for over a hundred miles in the direction she had headed. The Hummer's engine was still warm, so there was a chance the woman might be alive. Remounting his paint, he followed the tracks, doing what the tall, muscular breed did best – reading the land.

The weak winter light was fading as the temperature plummeted when Hawk came upon the still form. A less observant man would have missed her altogether, but his sharp, steely blue eyes caught a flash of red in the blowing snow. Reining in, he dismounted and squatted next to the diminutive shape. He removed one deer hide work glove, and gently brushed the snow off of the woman. Her red hair had spilled out of her hood and blown across the snow, or he may have missed her, as she was dressed entirely in military issue snow camo

Rolling her over, he opened her down jacket, removed his hat, and pressed his ear to her chest seeking a heartbeat. He was relieved when he found one. It was slow and weak, but steady. He walked over to the well-trained mount standing obediently with one rein dropped in the snow, and removed a Pendleton wool blanket from behind the saddle. After re-zipping the woman's jacket, he wrapped her tiny body in the blanket. Lifting her in his arms, he decided he was off by five pounds. She'd be lucky to weigh in at one-o-five with the heavy Pendleton, military issue pack boots, and all her clothes packed with snow. He must be losing his edge, he mused with wry humor.

It had taken a while to find her in the inclement weather, and with night coming on, it was going to take all of his formidable skill to keep them both alive. Alone and several hours ago, he and his paint could easily have made it to the line shack he usually used when riding fence. But now, with the temperature rapidly dropping, the wind rising, and the snow increasing, he was going to be hard pressed. After brief consideration, he decided it was still their best shot. With the child sized woman in his arms, he remounted the sturdy horse and headed north.

~

It was fully dark and the wind had stilled but the temperature plummeted to the sub zeros, and the stars were shining like diamonds when they finally reached the line shack. Hawk carried the alarmingly still woman inside and laid her on his bed. After lighting two kerosene lanterns, he fed the still smoldering coals in the wood stove with small sticks until they blazed back to life. He added increasingly larger sticks, finally topping them off with several, small split logs. Returning to his bed, he began removing the woman's outer clothing. While outside, they shielded her from the cold, inside, they would insulate her from the rising temperature in the cabin.

As he removed her jacket hood, masses of tangled red hair tumbled free. Some was frozen, packed in snow, so he was extremely careful not to break it off, as he knew could happen to wet hair in extremely low temperatures. After removing her outer wear and pack boots, he pulled off her wool pants and sweater, exposing thick, insulated underwear. Reevaluating, he decided she couldn't be over a hundred pounds on a good day after a full meal. He stripped off her neoprene underwear and discovered the first feminine articles of clothing—matching red lace push-up bra and thong.

Hawk stopped dead in shock. He had been about the business of doing what had to be done to save her life, so he was caught completely off guard. He found himself looking down at the most beautiful woman he'd ever seen wearing nothing but creamy skin and red lace undergarments. Her breasts were surprisingly full. Her waist was small, flaring out into curvy, toned hips and long shapely legs. Unable to stop himself, Hawk reverently ran the backs of his dark skinned fingers down her chilled ivory cheek, and a shockwave almost brought him to his knees. He felt his heart melt open and his cock turn to stone.

Mine!

Stunned to the core of his being, he quickly drew the covers over her and tucked her in, then stepped back from his bed – away from temptation. He had managed to distance his body, but his eyes wouldn't leave her.

Mine!

Suddenly he was terrified she wouldn't make it, that he would never see her open her eyes and look at him. He quickly returned to the bed, pulled back the covers and laid his ear against her breast. Her slow, steady heartbeat reassured him only marginally.

Hawk was not a man easily rattled. He was rattled now by his reaction to this woman, whose eyes he had never seen, voice he had never heard, and name he did not know.

He drew the covers over her, pulled more blankets from the ancient footlocker at the foot of the bed and wrapped her with them as well. Adding more wood to the stove, he put on a pot of water to boil, before reluctantly leaving her to tend his horse.

He unsaddled the exhausted paint, put him in the line shack's small barn and rubbed him down with practiced, efficient motions. Hawk broke the ice off the water trough, pulled off the paint's bridle, and left the horse with a substantial pile of hay and an extra measure of grain, only too anxious to check on the woman in his bed.

HIS woman in HIS bed!

WTF?

In all his thirty one years, he had never reacted like this to a woman. What was going on? It was not as if he was desperate for female companionship. He had just been to town last week.

Though he never seemed aware of it, with his high cheekbones, long black hair, copper skin from his Lakota mother's side, and six and a half foot, muscular frame and electric-blue eyes from his father's Nordic heritage, Hawk never lacked for female attention. Polite, quiet, mysterious, dark and dangerous, he drew women like flies. His cousins Nickolas and Daniel teased him unmercifully about all the besotted women that followed him around every time he showed up at the bar. Hawk would just smile indulgently, one large, long-fingered hand wrapped around his Pepsi, and his head tipped so the cowboy hat partially hid his bronze face. The cousins teased him about his choice of drink, too, but Hawk took it all in stride with quiet good nature.

He always assumed the women were really after his rich, good looking rancher cousins, and as ranch foreman, he merely reaped the rewards of association. Not that he begrudged them. He loved Nickolas and Daniel with a fierce loyalty. The brothers had defended the young, motherless Hawk when bigoted school yard bullies ganged up on him, beating him and calling him a "filthy breed". The only time anyone ever saw the giant of a man riled was when some hapless fool messed with one of his cousins.

Hawk entered the small one room cabin in his naturally silent way, and approached the bed in long, panther-like strides. Yup, she was still there – pale and unmoving. He could tell she was warming up some, as blood seeped from her thick red hair and dripped onto the pillow.

He sat on the edge of the bed and carefully pulled her hair back to examine the damage. She had a substantial cut in her scalp above the hairline. It was oozing blood and swelling as the room warmed her skin. He freed the leather thong from his hair, and used it to tie hers back so he could tend to her wound. Pulling dried herbs from a cabinet, he added them to the water warming on the stove, and returned to her side.

Her skin was still extremely cold to the touch, and she was still deeply unconscious. Gathering a clean rag from the sideboard, he dipped it in the tincture to make a compress, and gently covered the wound with it as he brushed stray red curls from her face with his other hand.

As his fingers touched her cheek, the shock of touching her blazed through his system and his Wranglers became uncomfortably tight in all the wrong places. He was an unredeemable pervert, he chided in self-disgust. Here she was, helpless, unconscious, wounded, half frozen and at his mercy, and he responded with a raging hard-on. What was wrong with him?

He lifted the cloth from her head to inspect the wound more closely. As he had feared, it would require stitches. Otherwise, it would become infected and scar. Resigned, he gathered his first aid kit from the cupboard and his straight razor from the sink.

Cutting off a small patch of her hair was excruciatingly painful for Hawk. Her hair should never be cut, he thought. It hung well below her hips in a glory of red curls, and to desecrate it felt like sacrilege.

He replaced the compress to the shorn area and gathered up the severed lock. Reaching under his shirt, he pulled out the leather pouch that hung around his neck, and placed the precious crimson mass into it. He replaced the pouch next to his heart, confused by his own actions.

It took him nearly an hour to suture her wound, but he wanted to get it perfect. The smaller the scar, the more her hair could grow back. By the time he was done she had started to shiver. While his mind understood the shivers were a good sign, indicating she was finally starting to warm, his heart could not stand to see her so. Hawk added more logs to the wood stove, shut down the damper for a long, slow burn, and stripped. He blew out the lanterns and climbed into bed with her, pulling her tiny freezing body to his, offering his warmth and comfort. Her shivering grew worse until she was almost convulsing, and he drew her more firmly into his embrace, holding her against his deeply muscled chest and praying she make it through the night. The wind rose, buffeting the cabin, as shivers wracked her tiny frame.

~ CHAPTER THREE ~

By the next morning, the wind increased and another front moved in, blanketing the sky and pregnant with snow. Hawk awoke with a warm, unconscious woman in his arms, and a morning wood pressed against her firm bottom, aching and twitching for entry.

FUCK!

YESSSS!

No, oh hell NO!

Hawk leaped out of bed in all his aroused glory, and looked down at the redheaded angel still unconscious in his bed. He hadn't thought it possible, but her ivory skin was actually paler than it had been the night before. There was no cell phone reception for miles, no motor vehicle access, and they were a full two days from the ranch by horseback – more than that riding double. Her life rested in his hands and, for whatever reason, his heart rested in hers.

FUCK!

For a man who never cussed he was sure catching on quickly.

As the day wore on and the storm worsened, Hawk knew he had to get her hydrated. Yet, she was unconscious and unable to drink. In a hospital, she would be given fluids intravenously, but this was no hospital. Vaguely remembering his Lakota mother tending him when he'd been very sick as a young boy, Hawk took water into his mouth. Pressing his lips over hers, he let it flow slowly from his mouth. Gently, he rubbed her throat and she swallowed. He repeated the maneuver until he felt she had all she could take, and then stoked the fire. She was shivering again without his body heat, so he joined her in the bed.

As afternoon turned to evening, Hawk dressed and went outside to draw water, gather firewood and tend his horse. He shot and cleaned a rabbit, and when he returned to the cabin, put it on the stove to boil, making a broth for his woman. When he approached the bed, he noticed her cheeks were flushed. He placed his hand on her forehead, bracing for the impact of touching her. Even though he thought he had prepared himself this time, his knees almost buckled as renewed desire rushed through him. She was hot to the touch, fevered and restless. At least she was finally moving – that had to be a good sign? Yet, the fever bothered him.

He checked her head wound but found no signs of infection. Pulling back the covers, he inspected her small body and found considerable bruising on her fair skin. The accident had taken its toll. The seatbelt injury was particularly troubling, indicating there was a strong possibility she had sustained internal injury along with her apparent concussion. Returning to the cupboard, he pulled out herbs and added them to the broth. His maternal grandfather was a medicine man and had taught him much. Hawk prayed he had learned enough. When the broth had cooled, he drew some into his mouth and fed it to his woman. Mouthful after mouthful he fed her, praying for her return to consciousness – her return to him.

The sunset was unremarked, blanketed by the still raging blizzard as Hawk battled for the life of his woman. Finally, as the grey light faded to full dark, she settled and he banked the fire, stripped and joined her in his bed, pulling her into his arms.

~ CHAPTER FOUR ~

She awoke blessedly warm. Long powerful arms held her back against a densely muscled chest. Long, thick hair, black and shiny as a raven's wing, blanketed her shoulder as soft warm breath caressed her neck. A heavy, hair roughened leg rested over both of hers from behind, pinning her to the gentle, warm bed. She could feel something hard, hot, and long pressing against the small of her back. For the first time in her life, she was in bed with a man – a fully aroused man, from the feel of it.

SHIT!

She turned and looked over her shoulder into the handsomest face she'd ever seen. Long black lashes fanned over blade-sharp, bronzed cheekbones. An abundance of black hair flowed over the pillow they shared, blending and tangling with her wild red locks. Big boned, muscular and dark-skinned, he looked like a pagan god.

"You are so screwed!" she rasped in her unused voice.

"Mmmm, not yet, ma'am, but a man can dream," he responded without opening his eyes.

"You don't understand, you can't touch me," she stated, panic clearly rising in her voice.

"Too late," the giant rumbled, pulling her closer into his warm embrace.

She pushed away, only to find she was weak as a kitten, and fell back to the bed, facing away from him.

"How did I get here?" she inquired quietly.

"Found you in a snow drift," he responded in his deep baritone. She could swear she heard humor in his voice.

"Where are we?"

"A line shack in B. F. Wyoming." This time she was sure she heard humor in his economical reply. She tried again to sit up to confront him, but her head began to pound as a wave of dizziness assaulted her.

"I'm going to be sick!" she informed him. That got some action. He leapt from the bed in all his massive naked glory, black hair flying, and brought her a pot just in the nick of time. He sat on the edge of the bed holding the pot for her use. He held her hair back with his other hand while she emptied the meager contents of her stomach, then fell back onto the pillow exhausted, arm cast over her eyes.

"You should have left me there. It would have been easier for everyone," she whispered from behind her arm.

"Nope, found you and I aim to keep you," he teased, trying to gauge her mental condition. At least he thought he was teasing, until he heard the truth and determination in his own words. She must have heard it, too, as she pulled her arm away from her face and gazed at him. Their eyes fused – his, startling blue in a bronze face; hers, unearthly starlit silver, set in ivory.

Hawk knew those eyes, God save him. They were the eyes of one of the prophesized Seven Sisters.

Now, here he sat, in the presence of one of the Seven Sisters with every cell in his substantial body screaming "*MINE*".

That she was his mate, he had no doubt. What to do about it, and how to proceed, was beyond him. A horrible thought struck. What if she wasn't his at all, but belonged to his cousin Daniel? Everything in him reared up in protest at the mere thought.

Mine! By. God. Mine.

Never before had he felt violent toward one of his cousins, but he was feeling more than violent at the thought of turning her over to Daniel. He had a very sick sense he would kill to keep her. She *had* to be his, that was all there was to it. There could be no other outcome.

Somehow, his rage was transmitted to the woman in his bed, as her eyes grew large and she tried to push up on her elbows in order to scoot further from him. He reached out and took her bare shoulder in his large calloused hand to prevent her moving and making herself sick again. She cringed at his touch, her eyes growing impossibly larger.

"Paslalyela Iyucanyankel pita," he soothed her in his native Lakota, much like he would a skittish horse.

"What did you say to me?"

"Steady little flame," Hawk translated, his dark face blazing in embarrassment. He hadn't realized he'd spoken in Lakota.

"What is your given name?" he asked, to cover his blunder.

At first, she looked puzzled. As more time passed without answering, she appeared alarmed.

"This is not a formal inquisition, little one, I just want to know how to address you," Hawk teased.

"I don't know," she whispered, eyes wide in horror. "I don't know my name. I don't know my own name," she repeated, shaking her head back and forth in denial, and trembling until she went into full blown convulsions and lost consciousness.

Hawk swept her into his arms and held her to his chest to prevent her from damaging herself in the seizure. When she finally stilled, she lay unconscious and virtually naked in his arms against his bare chest, with her soft bottom resting on his fully engorged cock.

"It's Okay, Iyucanyankel Pita," he said, holding her close. She may not know her own name, but he was finding he didn't know himself at all. Looking down at her innocent face, he wanted nothing more than to sink his raging body into her helpless one, and would gladly kill anyone who attempted to take her from him. He had counted himself an honorable man, only to find he had become a lecherous, homicidal beast.

He drew in the scent of her glorious hair as he gently rocked her back and forth. He continued to rock her, though he was uncertain whether it was she – or himself – he was attempting to comfort with the motion.

~ CHAPTER FIVE ~

Finally, she seemed to slip into a more natural sleep. He tucked her under the covers, gently smoothing her hair on the pillow. Hawk dressed, gathered the leather bundle holding his drum, and went out to greet the dawn in prayer as had his ancestors before him. He always greeted each day with prayer, and every sunset with ancient songs of gratitude, as his grandfather had taught him. This rising, he had much to pray for.

Facing the sunrise, he softly drummed and prayed for strength, wisdom, and courage. He prayed for the life and health of his woman, and the power to protect her. Should it turn out that she did not to belong to him, he fervently prayed for the strength and integrity to let her go. He closed with his power song before falling silent; face lifted to the sky, long black hair flowing down his back, patiently waiting – listening.

A noise, no more than a soft exhalation of breath behind him, drew his attention.

Standing, not three feet away, barefoot in the snow, and wrapped in his Pendleton blanket with her long red hair a banner in the wind, was his woman. There were no tracks in the deep snow leading from the cabin to where she stood, and her eyes were sightless, glowing like a thousand stars. The hair rose on the back of his neck when she spoke in many voices – gentle voices like falling rain – powerful voices like thunder.

"Nagi Canska, you are he who has been chosen. This Sister is yours to protect and to hold. It is this duty and privilege that makes you so volatile. This is as it should be, for she will need much protection and love in the times to come. Another has been chosen for your relation, so fear not losing her to him. Fear more, losing her to herself, for she has been broken. Seek not her old memories, but engage her new life. She is from the stars, yet this life has taken much from her. She chose death before she could remember who she truly is, necessitating her stellar identity to walk in prematurely. The stretch between who she was, and who she is to become, is great, causing her much difficulty. Care for her well, and walk in a good way, Nagi Canska, you are much loved among the star nations."

Her eyes closed, and she sank to the snow in a graceful swoon. Hawk lunged forward, grabbing her before she hit the ground, and lifted the unconscious woman into his arms.

Nagi Canska – Ghost Hawk. No living soul besides his grandfather knew his spirit name, yet she spoke it twice with perfect enunciation. As Hawk quickly strode back to the relative warmth of the cabin, he looked for signs of the woman's passing, but there were no tracks. He – the master tracker – could find no sign that she had ever left her bed. Yet, here she was in his arms, a good fifty yards from the cabin, in pristine snow bearing only the marks of his size twelve cowboy boots.

Other Books By

Cahira O'Donnell

THE LONG DARK NIGHT

THE SEVEN SISTERS SERIES
BOOK ONE

GHOST HAWK

THE SEVEN SISTERS SERIES
BOOK TWO
(COMING SOON)

CHALICE OF KARI

THE DAGURONIAN CHRONICLES
BOOK ONE
(COMING SEPTEMBER 2013)

ORACLE OF VIDAR

THE DAGURONIAN CHRONICLES
BOOK TWO
(COMING SOON)

.